Brayden

THE STANTON PACK BOOK 1

KATHI S. BARTON

World Castle Publishing, LLC
Pensacola, Florida
Copyright © Kathi S. Barton 2017
Paperback ISBN: 9781629896434
eBook ISBN: 9781629896441
First Edition World Castle Publishing, LLC, March 6, 2017
http://www.worldcastlepublishing.com

Licensing Notes
Cover: Karen Fuller
Editor: Maxine Bringenberg

CHAPTER 1

She sat up, then promptly leaned over and threw up twice. The first time she'd woken up, her head had hurt so badly she was sure something was stabbing her there. But one touch to her head had her fainting away again. Lying back down, she lay there trying to make the sick feeling in her head go away. Touching it gingerly, she felt the blood there again and the slice along her head, but there wasn't any memory of how it had gotten there. Nor — and this frightened her more than the head wound did — who or where she was.

Jane Doe. That's what she'd been referring to herself as since she'd awoken the second time. It had been dark where she first holed up. Not that the daylight she had now made things any clearer for her. Looking around from her position on the floor, she realized that she might be in some really old building that hadn't seen a broom or dust rag in a very long time. Slowly she rolled to her back, closing her eyes so she wouldn't get sick again.

"You need help, girl." She had also started talking to herself, she realized, and wondered if that was new or something she did all the time. Asking herself questions about the things she did know about herself didn't ring any bells either, but she listed them now. "You've been shot and wounded. You're female, and you're smart enough to know that hiding out was the best course of action for yourself. And you carry a gun."

She wrapped her fingers around the gun that hadn't left her side since she woke, and found it tucked tightly against her belly. It didn't feel foreign to her, but like something that she wore as routinely as she did a shirt or socks. There was a holster for it, but the gun hadn't been in it like it was now. Leather and steel, it had been strapped to her waist with one full magazine.

Searching for any kind of identification hadn't netted her anything. She had found a wound in her leg that had bothered her for a little bit, but not nearly like her head did. As she lay there, she thought of what could have happened to her and why. What was she that would make someone shoot her? Jane didn't want to think that someone was out to kill her, not yet at any rate.

"Was I a victim of a robbery gone bad? But if someone robbed me, wouldn't they have taken the gun too?" Her head began to pound again so she left that thought alone for now. "I need to get someone to help me. But who?"

Sitting up slowly, she felt her belly lurch again. Whatever had happened to her, it wasn't going to get any better by just sitting around waiting to have some sort of epiphany. She had a feeling that when she did recall what had gone down, she wasn't going to be any happier than she was with not remembering.

Standing was harder than sitting up, she soon discovered. Hanging onto the walls for support, her knees were weak and her hands shook. She could only hope that she was on a lower floor in the building, because she was sure that she'd never make stairs work for her. And when she saw them, all four flights, she sobbed like a baby. Nothing, she realized, was going to be easy about this. At least there was a handrail.

She had no idea how long it took, but she was on the last level when she heard cars. No people as yet...she'd not encountered anyone on her way down. She had to rest, so crawling behind the stairs, she found a nice cubbyhole and closed her eyes. It might be just a few feet from her, but freedom and perhaps answers were going to have to wait. She was simply too weak to walk even the few feet to the door. What if—and this had bothered her with each landing that she'd encountered—what if they were just waiting for her to come out so they could finish the job?

Darkness was coming on once again when she woke. She was getting sicker. Her belly was empty of whatever had been in it before, but it didn't stop her from throwing up. The bile was hot, and she was getting weaker each time she got sick. Help was going to have to come soon or she knew she'd be dead. Standing this time took her to the floor again. On her knees, all she could think about was that she was going to die, right here, and no one would ever know...if there was anyone to mourn her death. Lying down, Jane closed her eyes and rested.

It was nearing light again when she finally made her way out of the building. Her sleep had been fitful and unrestful, but she wasn't as sick this time when she moved. It was either because she was too far gone or she was getting better, which she doubted.

There wasn't anyone around except for a single truck that was idling nearby. As she staggered to the street, holding onto the walls as she went, she wondered who would be stupid enough to let a nice vehicle like that sit running unattended. Just as she was going to step out of the alley she was in, a slamming door had her turning to look.

It was too fast. Her head spun dizzily and she nearly fell again. As she held on to the overturned trash can beside her, she tried breathing in her nose and out of her mouth to slow the pain down, as well as to keep her belly from churning up again. For whatever reason the thought of being caught—at what she had no idea—but being caught or captured terrified her.

"Miss? Are you all right?" She wanted to scream at him that she wasn't fucking all right, but just nodded. "I'm sorry, but I don't think you are. Did you know that you're bleeding from your head and leg?"

"It won't stop. Every time I wake up, it's bleeding again." He might have said something, but she had to puke again and gagged twice before she laid down. "I think I'm dying."

"I'm going to call an ambulance." She screamed no at him, but must have blacked out for a bit. When she woke this time, she was in a moving vehicle. "You fainted, so I thought it was the perfect opportunity to get you to someone. But I won't call the police. I have no idea why I didn't, but I wanted you to know that."

"I don't know who I am." Trust. She didn't have any clue why she trusted this man, but she did. "I don't know where I am, how I got here, or how I was hurt. I'm at your mercy, it seems."

"Julian. Julian Stanton." She asked him who that was. "Sorry. Me. I'm Julian Stanton. I'm taking you to my home... well, to my parents' home. My father is a doctor. Retired now, but a good surgeon. I let him know what was going on about the wound, as well as that you seemed to be dead set against hospitals. He also knows that you're carrying."

She touched her fingers to the gun still in the holster. Touching it, like that man did, it gave her trust. Again, she had no idea why she did, but she laid her head back to rest. The trip didn't seem to take all that long, but she might have been out for a lot longer than she'd thought.

Three men were standing on the front porch when she

arrived at the house with Julian. Before he opened the door or they moved, he pointed out who they were. Two brothers and a father. Then when they moved toward her and the truck, she cringed when they started to reach for her.

"Let me give you something for the pain." The elderly man smiled at her. "It'll take you under for a bit, but that'll be fine while I exam you for injuries. You can trust us, young lady. We'll not harm you."

The pinch of the needle didn't hurt, but almost as soon as he rubbed the cotton ball over where he'd injected her, Jane felt herself floating away. It was the best she'd felt since she'd awoken. Flashes of light moved over her. Strong voices were there, but no words that she could understand. And on top of it all, a woman. Her kind voice made Jane feel like she'd been bathed in sunshine. Then there was nothing.

~~~

Denny waited for his wife, Lucy, to come and assist him while Julian filled him in on what had happened and why he'd brought her to their home. Denny checked the woman's head injury, and wasn't surprised to find it was a bullet wound. After cleaning it as gently as he could, he started to cut away her clothing. The gun perplexed him for a few moments, but Colton, his other son who had helped bring the young lady in, removed it from her and said he'd put it in the safe for her. Next, Denny removed her shoes, socks, and another weapon inside those. Whoever she was, she was well armed.

"I just heard from a man by the name of Wexton. I believe he runs the grocery store...or perhaps the library. They're all running together lately. Anyway, I have no idea why he'd think we have anything to do with this, but he said that someone is camping out in one of the buildings in the market district. I said that Julian checked it out today and it's nothing." After Lucy

9

pulled on gloves, she stood over the young woman. "Do we know anything?"

"Not as yet. At least not much. GSW to the head, but I think there will be more. There is blood on her pant legs as well as her hands. I was just going to take a look now." She helped him pulled off the tattered clothing he'd cut away. He noted the wounds they found as they took off her shirt. "Bullet on her shoulder. It looks like it might have been done before the other things, superficial. There is some bruising on her belly; boot print, it looks to be."

Denny, with the help of Lucy, rolled the young woman to her side. Her back was covered in scars that looked as if she'd been beaten, and repeatedly. There were a few more markings, none that he could recognize right off the top of his head. But as there was nothing life threatening, he moved to her pants. His wife took over there for him so that he could stitch up her head. He was just starting when he felt Lucy's fear and stepped back from his patient.

"Denny, what is that?" He looked where she was pointing, careful of his hands. He had to look at it very hard until what it was came to him. He took another step back and tried to think beyond the fear. "Tell me."

"I've not see this mark on someone in.... I was a boy and my father had been working with one of the women in the village. He said that she was the devil's handmaiden. Of course, as a child I believed him. But later, after doing some research, I found out that they're people marked by another tribe...that they were supposed to be unworthy." She asked him of what. "I don't know. That's all I could find. If she's been marked like this, Lucy, she might be older than she looks. I mean, as in decades older."

"What is she doing around here?" He said that he didn't

know. "Well, we'll fix her up, get some answers, and if we don't like them, we'll take care of her."

"Take care...what do you mean, take care of her? You're not suggesting that we murder this poor child, are you?" She just stared at him with that look she reserved for their sons. "Lucy, explain yourself, please."

"Take care of her as in taking care of her. Make sure that she's safe, well, and fed. Whatever made your mind rush to us killing her off? My goodness, Denny, you need to stop listening to those stories on the television set. Goodness gracious."

He said he didn't think it was that but a book he'd been reading, and moved to finish her head. "I knew I shouldn't have gone to bed straight away after reading that book. I swear to you, Lucy, that author has some chilling thoughts going on in his head." She told him to not read it at all. "It's good. I want to finish it, but perhaps I'll read only in the daylight hours. Not so close to bedtime."

They worked on her for over two hours. Under each article of clothing they removed they found more cuts and bruises. Another gunshot wound in her leg had startled him. Denny wondered why the young woman was still alive the way she'd been treated. As he was wrapping up the wound on her leg and setting it in a temporary cast to make sure it wasn't bumped, the woman looked at him.

"Hello." She nodded, but he thought her too weak to do much more than stare at him. "You've lost a lot of blood so I'm giving you some fluids. The wound on your head is stitched up, but I'm concerned at how deep it is. Julian told us you don't know who you are."

"No." She closed her eyes and he thought her asleep again. "I don't know anything. Where am I?"

"Stanton Ranch." She asked him what state. "Ohio. You're

11

just outside of Zanesville. My family and I have a nice ranch here. Not that we have much in the way of animals any longer, but we did a long time—"

"I had a gun. Where...did you take it?" He told her what one of his sons had done with it. "I'd like it back please. It...I have no idea why, but it comforts me."

"All right. But I'd like to wait until you're a little stronger. I've given you something for the pain, and I'd hate for someone to be hurt when you were out of it." She nodded, then moaned. "I've taken care of the wounds on your body. You have one GSW to the head, another to your shoulder, as well as one in your calf. They're cleaned up and stitched. I've saved the bullets for you."

"I don't know what I do for a living. I might be a bad guy." He'd thought of that as well, but had a feeling that wasn't what had gotten her shot. "The man who brought me here, you said he was your son. Will he tell anyone where I am?"

"No. He said you were inflexible about not going to the hospital, so he thought it might be safer for all of us not to tell anyone that we'd found you, nor that you were shot." She nodded again and Denny thought for sure she was out this time.

As he and Julian moved her to the bed he had set up in his offices at home, he asked him about what he thought had happened. He told him what she'd said to him when she woke up.

"You think she's a bad guy? Or anything to do with things that go bump in the night?" Denny told his son that he didn't. "I don't either. She could have shot me when I came up to her at the warehouse. Granted she was weak, but I think if she were a corrupt person, she would have done it anyway."

After moving her, he sat down at the little desk that was part of each room. He didn't use his offices much anymore…just for an occasional bump or two from one of the ranch hands. They only had a couple horses now, having sold them off a while back when he realized that he was just too old for ranching. His sons were off on their own now and Denny was proud of each of them, but he missed them when they weren't home. He supposed it was a way of life for the elderly.

Denny did a search on shootings in the area. A couple had occurred which were, he thought, too far away for the young woman to have traveled from. There was a robbery, but he wrote that off as well, knowing somehow that she might not have been involved in that either.

When Lucy brought him lunch on a tray they ate together, talking quietly about the upcoming picnic they were having, as well as Brayden's birthday. He was a little old for having parties, but it never stopped them from having them for their boys. However, they no longer hired a clown to entertain them.

"Do you suppose that he'll even be home this year? Last year he was two days late coming home." Brayden hadn't been home as much as they liked, not for years now. "I miss him more all the time. I know that he's working, but I'd so much like to have him home again."

"I've spoken to him a few times over the last few weeks. I guess things in Africa aren't going as well as they had thought, and he might be able to get away for a little longer this time. Something about money troubles, as well as supplies coming up missing." Lucy said that it would be nice to have him home. "I know, but when I talked to him, he sounded so beaten. Like he's just tired of it."

"Well, he's been working at building homes all over the world for others for nearly ten years now. I know as well as you that if you don't take a break now and again, you can't just pop back like you did before. He needs to come home and be with his family, and let someone else work for a little while. Perhaps he would do better at making money. Not that we need it, but I want him home occasionally." Denny agreed, but he wouldn't tell Brayden that. The boy was too stubborn about people telling him what to do. "When did he say he'd be here? Soon?"

"In a week. I had to make him narrow it down so that we could pick him up at the airport when he arrives. But of course, then I had to tell him several times that we didn't mind going out of our way to get him. I swear, Lucy, I think he does that to make me mad." She laughed and said they were alike in that. "What's that supposed to mean? I'm not aggravating."

"If you say so, love. But when you get something in your head, you're like a dog with a bone. You'll pick at it to death." They both looked over at the bed when the woman moaned. "She's going to make it, isn't she? I mean, she won't get weaker from this, correct? Poor thing. I wonder if whoever did this to her even cares."

"No, I don't think so. I have no idea why, but I think they would be upset to know she's alive. But we might have some trouble keeping her down until she heals more. And she's asked for her gun back and said that it's comforting to her for some reason. She seems stubborn herself, don't you think?" Lucy pointed out that she'd not spoken to her. "That's right. I forgot. I'm concerned about the marks on her back. What they might mean to her. Or us."

"I was going to ask you if you looked them up while you were down here, but for some reason I have it in my head for you not to. It might lead someone here." He nodded, telling her that he'd thought the same thing. "We don't know anything about her, Denny, but I want to protect her like she's our own child. Why is that, you suppose?"

"I don't know. But now that you mention it, I feel the same way. And even Julian said that he had this overwhelming need to make sure that she was safe. Not well, but safe. I asked him why and you know what he said? He told me that she needed him, that he felt it."

When she left him again, taking the tray with her, he sat at his computer to play a game. It was silly, he knew, when there were plenty of game systems upstairs, but he loved solitaire and found himself thinking about the game more than what he'd been doing earlier. It was a way to ease his mind...he had been playing games as a way to relieve stress for over a decade. The computer made it so much nicer.

When a small ding alerted him that he had an incoming message, he clicked on it to see what his son had to say now. Brayden had better not be changing his mind. He wanted his boy home. When it came up, he read it three times to make sure that he'd not misread it.

"I'm coming home, Dad. For good. I've had enough." He started typing a reply when a second message from him came up. "Would you find me a house? Not too big, but nice. With a pool. I find that I want to swim again."

He told him he'd do just that, and smiled as he wrote the rest of his answer. "Are you sure you don't want to build one? You should be good at it by now."

"I just want to live somewhere that is a nice home without any work on my part." Denny watched the little icon that said Brayden was still typing paused. When it came up on his end, Denny could only stare at it. "I'm getting married. After I'm home. She's not my mate, but I need some stability in my life and she can do it, I think. At least I hope so. She's a little on the.... You'll understand when you meet her. I'm bringing her home with me so you all can all get to know her too. Don't tell

15

Mom yet. I want to surprise her."

He'd certainly do that, Denny thought. Not his mate, yet he was going to marry her? That made his own cat sort of curl around him in fear. It was a feeling, one that had made him become a great surgeon, that had him thinking that his eldest son was about to make the biggest mistake of his life.

"We'll talk when you get here, son. Tell me when you expect to be at the airport and I'll be there." He told him he should be in the United States in two days. To pick him up on Wednesday. "All right. Give me times when you get them and I'll make sure that you and your lovely bride-to-be have a ride home."

Brayden said that he loved him and then the message box told him that he'd logged off. Denny checked on his patient then went to find his Lucy. There wasn't any way that he was going to keep this from her, and he found that he didn't want to. He needed someone to tell him he wasn't nuts for feeling this way.

"She's not his mate? You're sure that's what he said." Denny assured Lucy that he'd read it three times to be sure. "Why would he do a fool thing like that? Doesn't he know what sort of trouble that can cause him when she does come along?"

"He said he needs some stability in his life. And while I can understand that, I wonder if he knows he's not going to get it. Do you think he gets what he's doing?" She just huffed, something that she'd done all their married life when she thought he should know the answer to something. "Lucy, he's bringing her home to meet us. Oh, you're not supposed to know. He told me not to tell you."

"Well, I'm glad that you did. And no, I don't think he understands what he's doing. I can understand living with a woman if you're lonely. I don't care for it, but I guess I can

16

understand. But this is at a whole new level of living with someone for sex." Denny nodded, thinking that his wife was losing her filter more all the time when it came to talking about things. "Denny, you're going to have to talk to him as soon as he gets home."

"I will, I promise. But I'd like to say something to you, and I don't want you to get upset. You've been a little...how should I say this? You've been a lot more outspoken lately. Is it that club you've joined? The Women Over Fifty Group?" She kissed him on the cheek as she walked by him. "Lucy, you didn't answer me. What is it about you lately?"

"I've decided that I'm too old to be trying to please everyone." He said that he could understand that. "And I'm not saying what I want, I just have opinions. A great many of them. But I've been too shy to say them. I've decided that I'm not going to sit in the back row any longer, but voice my opinion."

After she left him in the kitchen, he laid his head on the butcher block they used as an island. Oh Lord, she was going to be the death of him, he just knew it. He smiled as he lifted his head. But she sure was fun now. He thought he liked this new Lucy. Going to the basement again, he sat with his patient.

Maybe, he thought, he'd take up this new habit Lucy had adopted. Saying what he wanted might be fun. Yes, sir, he was going to do that from now on instead of what people wanted to hear. He wondered what his sons would think about their new parents.

CHAPTER 2

Brayden realized his mistake the moment that the plane took off. He wasn't going to make it without saying something. The woman beside him, the one he was planning to marry when he got back home, was driving him nuts. More than that, she was irritating him so badly that all he wanted to do was throw her from the plane while it was still in flight. He shifted in his seat away from her when she laid her head on his shoulder. Again.

"I'm exhausted." He was too, he wanted to point out, but didn't. "I think that with your money, you could have gotten us home in a jet. I know that we'd be more comfortable. You act as if your money isn't important, but you do know that it is, don't you, Brady?"

"I don't think we would have been in the air any less time, Vonda. The flight is just as long in anything that we might have used. As for comfort, I'm sure that you'd like it less than you do this plane. Not to mention, I don't have a jet and more than likely never will. They're a waste of money." He tried his best not to tell her to get off him, but she was making that noise again. Grinding her teeth like it was a job and she was getting paid for being the best at annoying the fuck out of him. Why had he ever thought this was going to work? He needed a breath of air. Fresh air that she wasn't breathing. "I'm going to the bathroom."

"I'll go with you." He looked at her. "We'll have some fun in there. People do it all the time. And maybe we can have an announcement in a few weeks about making your parents grandparents. Wouldn't it be wonderful to have a child or two around for them to babysit?"

"No, we won't. I told you, there won't be any children from us." She put out her lower lip and he wanted to sock her in it. "I told you, Vonda. Several times. We won't have children. Not ever." He didn't tell her that they could adopt. He was having a hard-enough time just being around her...he could not imagine having a little baby in the mix too. Brayden couldn't believe the colossal mistake he'd made with her.

"I know, Brady. So you said, but you also told me that you'd not been fixed, so it still might happen." He shook his head. "Oh Brady, you know that we could have babies if you wanted. I do. At least two. A little boy and a little—"

"It's Brayden, not Brady. Vonda...." He let out a long breath. "Vonda, you're tired and not listening to me. I think that once we get home we'll be all right, but I'm holding back some things I want to say to you so that...I don't want to hurt your feelings."

She did that lip thing again. Had she always done that? What did it mean? She wasn't the woman that he'd found intriguing back at the job. That woman had been sweet, agreeable, and most assuredly not this whiney woman who seemed to have a one-track mind. Well, two track. If it wasn't his money it was having a child, both of which she was never getting. There was a prenup with her name on it as soon as they got to his house. He'd asked Christian to write it up for him.

Brayden stood up and didn't wait for her to come down the long aisle with him. As soon as he could, he went into the bathroom and locked the door behind him. Brayden looked at himself in the mirror and thought about Vonda Hull. What had he done?

Brayden had thought of himself as a level-headed man, at least most of the time. He didn't make rash decisions, nor did he do anything without a great deal of planning. He had planned, right down to proposing to Vonda, like a check list. He'd done all the background checks on her. He'd even had someone follow her around, without her knowledge of course, until he was sure that there was nothing hidden from him. Then they'd boarded a plane and she'd become...something else. Someone that he didn't care for. And now all he wanted to do was get out of this arrangement with his self-respect. She had belittled and pissed him off more in the last ten hours than anyone ever had before.

When someone knocked on the door, he finished up. Letting his body relax and his mind settle, he opened the door to find Vonda there. When she tried to shove him back into the bathroom, he stood his ground and asked her what she was doing.

"You seem so tense. I thought that I could get you relaxed. With my mouth." He looked around when someone snickered. "Come on, Brady. Let's have some fun. What else can we do up here?"

"Stay in our seats."

He moved by her and made his way to their area. Once she had flopped in her seat, no other word for it, he sat down as well. Stretching his neck, he heard it pop twice before he turned to look at her. She was staring out the window and he knew she was pissed.

Brayden started to apologize to her and realized that he'd done nothing wrong. And frankly, he was tired of saying he was sorry to her. Since they'd boarded yesterday, the first part of the trip on a long one home, he thought he'd said it to her a hundred times.

He'd found himself apologizing for the food that she'd been served that she'd ordered. For the way that the seats seemed to make her back hurt. How the drinks that she had been served were made with cheap liquor. Even the pillow that she'd been given on the flight to rest on was subpar and not to her liking. And through it all, he had told her he was sorry. Well, he was done. As of right now.

Closing his eyes, he tried to think. To let the past few hours settle over him so he could analyze them. Brayden decided that the things he was irritated with her about were more than likely due to boredom. He wasn't so much bored as he was exhausted. It had been a hellish six months, and he was ready for a good bed and a hot shower. Neither of which he'd used a lot lately due to the situation that he'd been working in.

When the announcement was made that they were landing in thirty minutes, he sat up. He must have fallen asleep, which didn't surprise him. He felt like he'd been run over a few times. Brayden felt better, his body rested enough that he felt that he could face Vonda again. But when he looked to her seat, not only was she gone but so were her things. Standing up, he found her at the back of the plane sitting with a man and woman that he didn't know.

Sitting back down, Brayden started to gather his things, trying his best not to be upset that she'd just go off with strangers and not stay with him. Logically he knew that he'd been sleeping, and more than likely had been for a few hours, but she'd left him. As he got his things packed up, he leaned back and let the last few days wash over him again. It was then that he realized he really wasn't upset that she'd left him, but was sort of relieved instead. And that made him feel bad.

A month ago he'd been working with a few of the construction workers on the last row of housing. They had worked together before, all of them, and while not best friends, they were friends. He had mentioned to one of them that he was going home soon and the man, Bill, had looked shocked.

"I thought you'd be staying on for a year or so yet." He asked him why he'd say that. "The future missus, she was saying that you two were going to have a baby soon."

"She's not pregnant." Bill said he knew that, but that was what she was telling his wife. Bill and his wife were cats as well. "You know as well as I that she's not my mate. And I've explained to her that we won't have children, but she keeps insisting that she might."

"Yes, I get that, but does she know why you're not having children? My wife seems to think that Vonda believes that she's going to be able to change your mind about having a child or two." Brayden said he was waiting until they got to his family home to tell her. "Probably a good idea. But I think you should be careful of her."

"Why is that?" Not fear, but something tingled along his spine. He had only proposed to Vonda the week before this conversation, and he didn't want to feel these emotions now. "Why are you thinking I need to be careful of the woman I'm going to marry?"

Instead of answering him, Bill told him to call his wife. Even gave him the number where she could be reached. Brayden wished now that he'd done that, called her to see what the issues were. Brayden hated the feeling that he was being taken. And now this, her being adamant about having a child.

Before the seat belt sign was turned on, Vonda came back to their seats. Brayden didn't comment on her leaving him, nor the fact that she smelled strongly of alcohol. After she made sure that she had all her things, including her phone, he sat quietly next to her. He wasn't going to get into it with her now.

"You could have at least asked me where I've been." He told her that he'd seen her back there and assumed she was just having some fun. "I was, actually. It was nice to be able to talk to someone that wasn't biting my head off all the time. I don't think I like this angry you."

"I'm sorry you feel that way, Vonda." And he was too. For a great many things, but mostly for him thinking he could make this work with this nutball. "I needed to sleep. I've been running for the last week on just a couple of hours of rest a night. I think that's why I've been so short."

Again with the lip, and he decided that he wasn't going to think about how she thought that puckering her lip out like she did was going to get her anywhere. When he asked her if she was ready to meet his family, she shook her head.

"Why don't we stay in town tonight, and go out to see them in a couple of days?" He started to tell her that he'd not seen them in six months and needed them. "We could rest up. You can take me shopping, and we'll have extravagant meals every night before going to the farm."

"It's a ranch, not a farm, and my family is waiting for us. My mom said she was making my favorite dinner." He looked away when she started the lip movement again. "Besides, I've already told my dad we were landing soon, and he's there to pick us up."

Brayden reached for his dad then, completely forgetting about his promise to call him when they were ready. His dad was waiting for them, but not at the airport. He was laughing as he told him that they were in town and would be delighted to get them.

Vonda, the woman I brought here, she's not excited about

meeting you. I think she's kind of nervous. His dad said he could understand that completely. *We've been traveling for three days too. I know that I've been a little short with her, so if she gives you the first wrong impression, that's it.*

He didn't want his dad to know his true feelings. That he'd fucked up, that deciding to marry this woman had been a stupid idea. Brayden wanted to talk to his dad, but knew that now wasn't the time.

His dad was quiet for several seconds and Brayden closed his eyes again, waiting for his dad to tell him he was making the mistake he'd already figured out. He'd not made such a bad one that it was irreparable, but he felt more and more of late that he was getting there. There wasn't any way that he could feel good about marrying Vonda. Brayden was afraid that he was waiting for validation from someone so he could stop this.

Well, if you'd rather wait until tomorrow night to have dinner, your mom said she could put it off for you. Everything is about ready, but that's all right with her. Brayden said it would be great tonight, he was excited about seeing them all. *Good. I was hoping you'd say that. We have a guest at the surgery, by the way. I'll explain it to you when you get here. I'm so glad you're coming home, son. You have no idea.*

He was excited too. And relieved. His family was there for him, as he'd known they would be. Brayden had missed them as well, all of them, and was glad that he was finally home.

Eventually the things that he'd left undone in Africa would need to be dealt with, but not now. Not right away anyway. He had left in a hurry, he knew that, but it was for the best...he knew that as well.

When the pilot announced to them that it was ten minutes until landing, he told his dad. His parents were still about twenty minutes away, but he figured by the time they got their

25

luggage and made their way out of the terminal, even as small as it was, they'd arrive. Brayden felt himself relax and a smile filled his face. He was home, that was all he could think about right now.

~~~

Jane looked around the pretty little room. She wasn't ready to move yet, or to even ask the man sitting at the desk near the door any questions. For some reason, she thought he knew she was looking at him, but he, for whatever reason, decided to just let her. Slowly she rolled to her back and tried to breathe through the pain.

"Near your right hand is a small button on a cord. If you press it, it'll give you some medication to ease your pain." Nodding, she reached for and found what he was talking about. "You can press it seven times, I think Dad said, before it gives you a full dose of medication. But he said that you should lead up to that if you can."

She pressed it twice. The second time had been an accident, but almost as soon as she turned to look at the man again, she realized that it was working for now. The pain was tolerable but not gone, which meant that she could talk.

"How long have I been here?" He got up and moved to the chair that was near the bed. He looked like the first person she'd seen, but not quite. "I don't know you."

"We were introduced, but I think you might have been in too much pain to remember. I'm Colton. My dad is the surgeon. Julian, he's the one that brought you here." He moved to the desk, then came back to her and put her gun in her hands. "My dad said I was to give you this as soon as you woke for more than two minutes. It's been longer, but you didn't move so I waited."

Curling her fingers around the handle she felt better. Not

out of pain, but just better. As he sat down again, she wondered at her question about how long she'd been here. He smiled.

"Ten days. Dad removed the bullets and stitched you up. Right now, your leg is in a temporary cast just so that it can heal without splitting open the stitches. Also, he thinks you have some muscle damage to your shoulder, but he said with a little work you should be able to have full use of it in no time. I told him that I thought you'd have it in half of what he said, but he didn't take the bet." She asked him why he'd say that. "Because I have a feeling that you're the kind of person who enjoys proving people wrong about yourself."

"I don't know anything about myself, not even what happened to me." He nodded. "I'm assuming that you've been doing some research on what might have happened?"

"Actually, I've been playing match games. Dad and I have this thing…we relax by figuring out puzzles and other mundane games. It takes our minds off whatever might be boiling around in our heads. How do you relax?" The question was innocent enough, but she had an answer.

"I do Sudoku." He grinned. And she realized that it *was* something that she did. A memory. Watching him, she figured that he had been looking her up somehow. "How did you do that? I mean, you did something that made me remember that."

"No. I just got you relaxed in your head and then asked. No pressure on your part, but it tells me that there wasn't any permanent damage done to you that caused your loss of memory." He told her that when she was better, he'd get her some puzzles. "Don't try to remember things. Just let them come to you naturally. I mean, say you're in the kitchen and someone says to you that we're having liver and onions for dinner. You might know if that's something that you like or dislike. Though I can't think of a single thing that would be good about the stuff. Nasty. But that's just me."

She wasn't sure on that one. Her mind was working hard at trying to figure it out when he started talking again. Jane had a feeling that he was trying to help her, but she felt her head start to ache again. And then there was a pain in her chest, like someone was trying to squeeze out all the air she had in her body.

"Just breathe, okay?" She nodded, but could feel the pain getting the better of her. She was gasping at air, any amount so that she could just breathe. "You're thinking too hard. Just.... Here, look at me."

She did, and he was so close to her face that she moved back and felt the searing pain of the wound in her head. But the feeling of pressure in her chest was gone. Jane looked at him sharply, thinking that he was cruel.

"You need to breathe deeper. That's it. Be angry, but just breathe." The pain in her head started to fade, and that was when she realized he was drugging her. "Just another punch to the meds and you'll be all right. Just breathe. In and out. I'm sorry that I hurt you, but you were panicky and that's not good for anyone. Breathe."

She was beginning to feel drugged. As her eyes grew heavier, she grabbed his arm and held him. The feeling of sinking below the water line was going away, to be replaced with the feeling of helplessness.

"I don't know me." He said he knew that and told her it would come to her. "I'm afraid someone is coming for me. I don't know why or who, but I feel that. And you've been so kind to me, but I have a feeling that when they find me, they'll hurt you as well."

"Then it's more than likely true. It also might be what is keeping you from remembering much about how you got in

28

this condition." She nodded, her eyes feeling heavier. "Just let yourself go. No one here is going to hurt you. We're keeping you safe."

"No one has done that for me before." He told her that she was in good hands now. "I'm not human. I don't think you are either."

Jane had no idea where that thought had come from, but she knew it to be true. Though what she was, she didn't know, only that she wasn't like normal people.

"You're right, neither are we. I'm a cougar. And you are?" She said she didn't know, only that she wasn't human. "Good to know. So, you let the drugs take you to la-la-land and someone will be here when you wake. My mom, she's made some broth for you, and if you want it later, I'll see that you get it."

"What are you?" He said cougar again. "No. I mean, you're a doctor, aren't you? You know what I'm going through."

"Yes, a doctor of psychology. I'm a psychologist. I'm a head doctor." She felt herself being taken under stronger then, her entire body just going limp. But a thought touched her mind, a small one, and she said it before she went under.

The dream, or whatever it was, started out in the building that she'd been in. There were differences…slight ones, but she could see them. There were rats in the corner that hadn't been there before. The windows were open and she could feel the breeze. She wasn't sure that the floor that she'd been on had any windows. And there were voices.

Jane moved closer to them. They were sharp, loud, and male. She thought that she should know the men behind the wall that separated them, but didn't know them as yet. When she could finally make out what they were saying, she paused by the opening.

Other things occurred to her then. She was dressed

differently. While before she had on a pair of dark pants and a black tee, she now had on jeans and a jacket. Her gun was there, but she thought that it was different too, and realized that it was silenced. She listened as the two men spoke to each other.

"I thought you said you had someone on him at all times." The other voice laughed and Jane leaned against the wall. "What do you think is so fucking funny? Even with the kind of money we might make off this deal, we can't spend it if we're dead."

"I told you, several times as a matter of fact, that I have it under control. Things are going smoothly now, and it should only be a couple more days before we have him right where we want him." The first man asked where that would be. "You just concentrate on keeping the police out of our business and we'll be just fine."

"You know as well as I that they're nowhere near this. No one has a clue what we've got going. I've made sure of that." Jane pulled out her phone and turned on the recorder. Whatever was said now, she'd be able to listen to it all later. "You just make sure that things are set up on your end when you call me. If not, then don't even bother looking me up. I'm going to be gone long before they can attach my name to yours."

"You do that." The second man laughed as he continued. "Oh, I heard of that guy again, the one that you told me to watch out for. Where is he in the scheme of things?"

"Dane? Don't even know what this guy looks like, much less whether or not he's going to be a team player. I just heard that he's been taking over some of the area around the campus and making a name for himself. He works for the big guy, and we'll have to deal with him if we want to make any money. I've also heard through the grapevine that he'll be joining forces soon with Sams. That's why we need to get this done before he arrives. I don't think we're going to be able to pull the wool over his eyes for very long. Not with this Dane person hanging around."

The second man laughed again, the sound of it grating and familiar. "I'm not worried about somebody that may or may not be a threat to us. We've been planning this for far too long for some upstart to come in and fuck it up for us." She heard paper rattling. "Here is the money that you'll need to grease some palms. Remember what I told you…don't think about the amount, but how much it's going to help us be the boss."

The voices faded away, but Jane had a feeling it was more to do with her than the fact that the men had stopped talking. This time, in this dream, she was sitting at a large table with two people that she couldn't make out. Not that they were unfamiliar to her, but they were blurred for some reason.

"Do you know what they'll do if they find you?" A voice like before, which she thought she should have recognized. "They'll cut you up into pieces and then sell those to the highest bidder. You must remain safe and out of the public eye."

"Yes." It was her voice, she realized, that answered. But it was full of confidence. Like she was cocky, or stupid. "I'll be safe and keep you that way too. We'll get this worked out, and then I can be on my own."

"If you don't and fail, we all die. They won't take it too kindly to find out that they've been had." She nodded at them, their faces still blurred from her. "We'll let you go, but you must remember that if anyone finds out about you, they find us all. And that will be the end of everything we've done to make it better."

Better how, she wanted to ask. Who were they working for that was going to get them killed? And why was it so important that she succeed? These were questions she had no answers to.

31

But that didn't stop them from forming.

The dream changed again, and this time she was dressed as she had been when she'd awoken. Her gun was out, her body hard with fear. As she lifted her gun up, to no doubt fire at something or someone, she saw the face in front of her. She knew them, that's all she could think. The person that she was going to kill, she knew them.

The bullet hit her in the head, knocking her to the ground. Another ripped through her arm, then her leg. As she was crawling away she heard them, the men from the other room. They were screaming at her, or for her. But it made no sense to her. They were screaming for the person that the other men had been talking about. Screaming for Dane.

CHAPTER 3

Lucy watched her son and the new girlfriend. They were so totally unsuited that she was surprised that no one mentioned it to him. Of course, it could have been because the girl, Vonda, wouldn't let him out of her sight, nor her clutches. Lucy had never seen a more pathetic woman in her life.

She was for sure the clingiest thing she'd ever seen. Cougars weren't a pack sort of group, but she had to hand it to Brayden, he was sure more tolerant than she might have been. Lucy thought she should try and separate the two of them, even if only to give her son a break. He looked as if he might need it.

"Brayden, I was wondering if you could come on down to my clinic. I have a few things down there that aren't working the way that they should. I know I don't use them much, but I would still like to know that they're in working order." Lucy looked at her husband and smiled. When he winked at her, she knew that he'd been thinking the same thing. "You won't mind, will you, Vonda? It won't take but a minute or two. Dinner will be called soon, and I'd like to get it done while I'm thinking about it."

"Oh, I could go too. You never know, I might have some input as well. I've been in doctors' offices before." Lucy could see the panic in Brayden's eyes. The boy was going to have to talk to her or she'd have to take him to the woodshed. Lucy intervened, but was going to have a serious talk with Brayden later.

"Why don't you come with me, Vonda? You can have a look at my garden. I've been raising prized roses for years now." She looked like she was going to turn her down. "You can pick out some of my blooms for your wedding."

She was out the door in front of her, and Lucy started to follow her out when Levi grabbed her hand. Lucy asked her son what was wrong.

"Lock her out. Don't let her back in the house, and maybe we can talk Brayden into not going through with this. She's.... He can't seriously think that she's right for him. Mom, she's insane. As much as I hate to say it, I think that she's as nutty as a box of nuts." Lucy said that apparently, Brayden did plan on going through with it. "My goodness. Well, that settles it, I'm never coming home again. Not if she's a member of this family."

"You'll do no such thing. He's your brother. And which one of you have made bad choices and still had the support of the rest of us?" She looked at five of her sons, and each of them raised their hands. "Now. We're going to be nice, civil, and we're going to be supportive. And pray to God he sees her for what she is."

By the time she made her way out to her gardens, Vonda was already picking them. Her heart nearly broke when she saw that she'd picked two of her blossoms off her prize-winning roses. Lucy told her to stop right now.

"I thought you said we're going to pick some for the wedding." Lucy pointed out that they weren't getting married today. "You never know. And soon, we'll be making you a grandma. Won't that be great? You can be our babysitter whenever we go out. And just because I'm going to be a mom, I don't plan on staying at home every night. Brady doesn't want children, but I think I can talk him into them. What kind of family would we be if there were no children?"

"It's my understanding that there won't be any children from this union." Vonda told her that accidents happened all the time. "I see. And this accident that you're talking about, are you saying that you're pregnant now?"

"Oh no, not yet at any rate. But soon Brayden will buy us a big house and fill it with nice things, then we'll have a child. I know that he says no now, but like I said, things can happen to make it true. He'll be a great dad, don't you think?" Lucy said she thought he would too. "And with his money, we can hire a group of nannies that can take care of them for us. And you, of course."

"You're very keen on his money." Vonda looked at her like she was confused. "I mean, you are talking like this marriage is going to bring you a great deal of wealth. I'm assuming he's discussed a prenuptial agreement with you, hasn't he? I believe that he's had his brother, Christian, draw one up for the two of you."

"Yes, he did mention that, but I don't think he's being all that serious, do you? I mean, I'm going to be his wife. And if something should happen between us, then he'll want to take care of me in a fitting manner, don't you think? He'll just have to tell Chris that he's changed his mind, that's all." She wandered through the rest of the garden. And when she turned to her, Lucy could see that the dumb act was gone. This was the real Vonda. "I'm not going to sign it anyway, even if he tells me to. I know what I want, and that isn't going to happen. Brady will marry me and we'll have a kid or two, because in the event that we divorce, then I'll have child support and the big house. I'm not as stupid as you believe I am."

35

"I would say that you are if you think things will go your way. And I also think that you're a manipulative person. But it will do you little good if you believe you're going to win against this family." Vonda said she already had. "If you say so. Now, I would like for you to go inside and out of my garden. And don't steal anything on your way out the door either."

As she walked by the roses, ones that she'd nurtured for years and years, Vonda stomped two of them into the ground. Lucy felt her cat stir. She wanted blood and this woman had better watch her step from now on. Going in behind her, she locked the door and told her husband what had happened.

Should I tell, Brayden? She asked if it would do any good. *It might. I'll be casual about it. Just mention that you're upset. My goodness, darling. What has he gotten himself into?*

I don't know, but he'd better figure it out soon enough. She plans on taking him to the cleaners if they divorce. She told him about the children and child support. *I'm assuming that he's not mentioned the fact that he's a shifter yet, has he?*

I'll have a talk with him. He might have his reasons. Though for the life of me, I can't figure out what they might be. Also, I'm going to check on our little girl while I'm here. We'll be up soon.

~~~

"I'm sorry, Dad." Brayden looked at the wall that his dad was telling him about and knew that his entire family had seen how upset he was. "I should have known better. I just thought...I have no idea what I was thinking when I decided to marry her. She's not the same woman that I proposed to. Not by long shot."

"I didn't think so. You have no idea how glad I am to hear that you didn't on purpose want to marry that...that thing." Brayden sat down. His dad did as well. "What are you going to do about this? I mean, you're not going to marry her, are you?"

"No. I mean, hell no. But I don't know what to do about her. She's got it in her head that we're going to have a nice wedding that I'll pay for. A big house, again that I'll simply buy for her, and that I'll give her children. I've told her at least a dozen times a day that there won't be children for us, but she's just not listening to me. Or she feels like she can talk me into something. The more I think about it, Dad, I swear to you, I believe she convinced me to marry her. Not entirely her fault, but I do feel that she planted it in my head or something." He got up and paced the little room. "I thought when we were coming here it was the stress of flying. But I've come to realize it's simply her. She is not a very nice person. And I've begun to just hate her."

"No kidding, son, she is a nasty person. She just trampled your mother's roses and you know how much she loves those things. And Vonda, I guess you could say that she let her true colors show while they were out there. She talked about the prenup and how she wasn't going to sign it. And that having a child with you would give her more leverage if she divorced you. She didn't say it exactly like that, but close enough that your mother is upset." Brayden nodded. Vonda had hurt him, but hurting his mom was more painful than anything. "I think your brothers are about to take her out and beat her to a pulp too. They don't care for her."

"Neither do I." He hated to admit to making such a massive mistake, but he had. "I'll fix this, even if I have to pay her off instead of marrying her. She's not going to take me, however. I should have seen that from the first. But, honestly, Dad, I'm so bored with life, I thought she might spice it up a bit for me."

"She'll certainly do that for you." They were both laughing as they headed to the stairs. "Oh. I have to check on my patient. You go on up and I'll be there in a bit. She's awake more now, so I want to check on her."

"Can I go as well? I'm not ready to face them yet." His dad said that was fine as he made his way to the suites that he used. "Dad, I truly am sorry about this. And I'll make it up to Mom about the flowers. I can't believe...I was going to say I can't believe some people, but with her, I can. Like I said, she is a monster and I'll be glad to be rid of her."

"She's all right with it. But it'll be better if you talk to your mom and tell her what you told me." He nodded as they entered the last room in the hall. "This is her. Poor thing. She's resting again. Colton spoke to her earlier and she is still having trouble— Brayden? What is it?"

He looked at his dad. This had to be a joke. One of them was playing tricks on him. This just could not be happening to him right now. His dad asked again if he was all right.

"Yes. Just fine. I was...I was just shocked at the extent of her injuries." Which was a lie and his dad probably knew it. There was nothing to see on the young woman other than a bandage around her head. "Did you say that she's lost her memory? That she doesn't know her name?"

"Yes. Colton got her to remember something by using some of his skills on her, so we know that it's not permanent. Also, she said something to him, something about Nelson Pharmaceuticals, but he didn't know what she meant. We're not looking things up about her because we have a feeling that she's in trouble with someone. Not sure who, but we're holding off to see if she remembers anything first. No sense in rocking the boat without an oar, you know." His dad continued to talk, but Brayden was no longer listening. He was afraid.

By the time they were at the stairs again, Brayden knew that this woman was his mate. But he didn't want to tell anyone until.... Well, he had to do this on his own. To figure out how to take care of Vonda and talk to this other woman. He was so fucked right now that he was somewhat sick to his stomach. And it was all his fault.

Had he just thought things through, perhaps given coming home a little bit of time before this thing with Vonda…. Brayden was lonely, he supposed, but it more than likely had more to do with him not being home than anything else. But he knew one thing for sure. Vonda was not going to be happy about this turn of events, not one bit.

Dinner consisted of all his favorites. There was prime rib, green beans, as well as baked potatoes. Homemade bread that only his mom made the way he loved it. Brayden also knew there would be an almost endless supply of iced tea, and cherry pie for dessert with fresh creamy ice cream. And if he didn't mistake the smell coming from the kitchen, there was peach clobber as well. After their plates were filled, he began to relax a little more. Having his family around helped a great deal.

There was talk of what they were all doing. Brayden had been gone for six months, and before that nearly two years with only about a month in between. He'd missed a great deal, it seemed, and he enjoyed listening to each of his brothers talking about their lives.

Christian was working hard at establishing himself as a country attorney. He'd been trying cases, as well as giving a few lectures at the local high school and community college. He was running his own office and taking care of a few judicial things at the town hall when needed.

Julian was taking it easy for now. He'd been put on medical leave about a year ago, and it seemed he wasn't in any hurry to go back. He'd loved being a beat cop, he told them, but thought that being a private detective might be more in line with what he wanted to do with his life.

His brother Colton loved what he did, and Brayden was sure that he'd be a psychologist for the rest of his life. He was good at it too, but said that soon he wanted to venture into helping children, those that had been abused by not just the system, but parents as well. Brayden thought there were far too many of the latter, but knew that Colton would be good at it.

The only one with any artistic talent was Levi. He'd been painting since he was old enough to hold a paintbrush. Now, Brayden learned that he'd branched out even more to include not just pottery, but photography as well. They set up a time for him to go and see his work later in the week.

Wyatt had followed in the footsteps of their dad. He was now a surgeon that was as well respected as their Dad, but Wyatt was fast becoming the go to man when there was something that needed delicate work. Brayden knew that Wyatt should be in a bigger city hospital where he'd have more work, but he was also glad that he was home with the rest of them.

"How much longer are we required to stay here?" He glanced around the room when Vonda spoke, too loudly he thought. "I mean, it's not like you have to be here for every little story, do you?"

"Yes. Yes, as a matter of fact, I do. If you'd like to go up to your room, then by all means, go ahead. I've missed them and I want to visit." She just stared at him, then turned in her chair so that her back was to him. Brayden was sure that she expected him to say something or even to give in, but he turned and spoke to his mom.

Mom winked at him and Brayden knew that he was going to have to talk to Vonda tomorrow. This had gone on long enough. Too long, actually.

His mind kept drifting to the woman downstairs. He knew that he'd not get any information from his family. He knew as much as they did since she had no memory of anything. But as soon as he could, Brayden was going to slip down and see her again. Just to make sure. Of what he wasn't positive, but he was going to go down and talk to her if she was awake. If not, he was going to enjoy the quiet after being with Vonda for so long.

"How long are you home for, Brayden? I sure have missed having you around. Please tell me it's going to be a while." Brayden started to tell Wyatt he was home for good when Vonda spoke.

"Oh no. We're only here to get married, then we're off again. We'll be traveling around a great deal, so it's doubtful that we'll be in one place for very long. After the honeymoon, I want to see how other countries live it up. Brady is a party animal." No one said a word. Then Wyatt started to laugh. "What's so funny? You don't believe me? He is. The night before we left that place, he had a great party and invited everyone."

"I'm curious...are you planning to let him say anything for himself? And who the hell is Brady?" Wyatt looked at him. "You? She calls you Brady? You hate that nickname. Why are you allowing her to call you that?"

"I've asked her several times not to, but she thinks it's funny. It's like she has this blockage with it or something. And about that party? Yes, everyone was there, but I didn't throw it. I was given a going away celebration and whoever stopped by was welcomed. I neither drank nor had any of the food. It was a going away thing, and whoever stopped by was welcomed." He looked at Vonda. "You weren't even there. How do you know what sort of party it was? You said you didn't want to go and hang out with good-for-nothings, if I remember correctly."

"I heard about it. And you're not very nice, Brady." He had embarrassed her. And her way of getting back at him was to try and humiliate him. She'd done it twice on the plane when she'd

41

brought up children again. "I wonder if your parents know how much you drink and what a lush you are when you're drunk. He's a bully too."

"I sincerely doubt that. I know for a fact that he doesn't drink, nor is he a bully." He watched his mom instead of Vonda as she continued. "You might want to stop with the lies, young lady. They'll get you nowhere with us. We've all known Brayden a good deal longer than you have. He might be an animal—we all are—but we're not the type that you've portrayed him to be. So either shut up or tell the truth. That stuff won't fly here."

"You're not very nice either. In fact, I think you're all very rude people, and I cannot wait until we're married and away from you. I can't stand any of you. Brady, I think it's time we headed up to bed. The sooner we can get out of here, the happier I'll be." No one moved when Vonda stood up and glared at his mom. "None of you have been very welcoming since I got here. When we're married, I'm going to make sure that you don't get to see him. How's that?"

"You won't keep me from my family." She turned and looked at him and pushed out her lower lip. "That won't work either. You're not going to manipulate or humiliate me in front of my family again, Vonda. I won't tolerate it."

He felt like the king of the world. For all of about two seconds. When she slapped him, hard enough to jerk his head around, he felt like a fool. Vonda had led him down this merry path, and now he felt bad that his family had to see it. When she turned on her heel and left the room, he sat there with his head down.

"I'm so terribly sorry. I know this is no excuse, but I swear to you, she was never like this before I proposed. She was sweet, kind, and never said a word that was disagreeable. Not where I could hear it at least." He looked around at all of them. "Then yesterday I made a phone call that I should have made before leaving there. I talked to the wife of a good friend of mine. She told me that she'd known Vonda for a long time and that she is a monster. I know that now. She shows that to me every time I'm near her. Each time she opens her mouth, I see it. I need to figure out a way to get her out of my life. I need your help, please."

"Thank goodness." He looked at Colton. "Christ man, she's a horrible person, and to be honest with you, I couldn't figure out how we were going to have dinners or any kind of family life with her around. I'm so glad that you've figured this out before it's too late. And I swear, if she tells me one more time that you two are going to have children, I'm going to cold-cock her."

"I asked her to marry me." Christian nodded and asked him if he'd gotten her to sign the prenup. "No, and she decided that she won't sign it until after a year of marriage. I told her, countless times, that without it there won't be one. Not that I'm going to marry her anyway, but she has to be insane if she thinks I would have let that slide."

"Let me have a go at her and maybe I can help you out with that. Not her signing it, but perhaps I can make a change or two to it that might have some bearing on it. I didn't think to put in it about children." He asked him what he meant. "As in, you tell her that any child born of her you won't claim. Flat out. I can put that in there for you before I speak to her. It might save you some heartache even if you don't marry her."

"I'll talk to you about it after dinner." Christian nodded and said he was staying in town for a couple of days, and would look it over when he got done with this case. "Anyone else have any suggestions?"

"I don't think I'd let her know that you're not human." He

asked Colton why that would be important. "Because I have a feeling that little Miss Hull would figure out a way to tell the world if you did. And if it happens that she needs to know, I'd make sure that she's nowhere that she can record your shift and that she doesn't have her camera on her when you do. I have a feeling that your secret might end up on social media long before she is out of your life."

"I had planned to tell her while we're here. I don't know why, but it felt safer." Colton nodded and said that it would have been. "I thought about that plan when we were coming home, and I can see that you're right too. I have a feeling that she's out to get whatever she can from me, and damn the consequences on my end."

"I'd say that's a fair statement." No one said anything when the door upstairs slammed. He wondered which room she was in and decided that he didn't care. His mom laughed. "She's in the far room at the end of the hall. And just now, I decided that you'd be more comfortable in the pool house. What do you think, son?"

"Anywhere that's as far from her as I can get. Thank you. All of you."

They each said it was their pleasure and Brayden had a feeling that they sincerely meant it. He didn't tell them what he'd discovered in the basement. He knew that they'd be happy, but they'd also be rougher on Vonda. And her being here was his fault. Brayden didn't want her to suffer any more than she had to while here. Though the more she acted out, the more he wanted to hurt her as badly as she had him and his family. The roses…that just tore him up inside to think that his mom's beautiful flowers were destroyed.

Brayden thought about going up to check on Vonda, but in the end, he stayed with his family, telling them about the problems that he'd had on the job site and how he'd been treated.

"I know that we were in a different country, but I'm telling you right now, some of those people over there, the ones in charge of the housing units we were putting in, they're going to fail soon if they haven't already. There is no money left and a great many unpaid bills. The first I heard of lack of funding was when someone came to me with one of them." Julian asked him what he said to the person. "That I wasn't responsible and he said that I was the one they were told to find for their money. And if I didn't pay them in full, there would be no more materials brought to the development. It was over ten grand. Way too much for the four houses we were putting up this time."

"I thought all the materials were donated. I mean, that's the only way you work this, correct?" He told his dad that it was how they'd been doing it all along. "Then how did a bill for that much merchandise even come to be? I think something fishy is going on, son, and you're well off breaking ties with them."

Brayden was an inventor as well as an engineer. He could come up with plans and execute them into working pieces in no time. It was how he made his money…going to places, seeing what needed to be improved over what was already in place, and making it work. He loved what he did, and enjoyed the excitement of making something work for them.

But his part in the building of homes for the needy was to figure out the materials needed to make the homes structurally sound, clean, and work well in the environment. Which, in the case of the homes he was helping build, meant it was resistant to heat and easy to maintain. A great many people lived without even the simple comfort of a bed that wasn't made from stone and grass. A home also gave them a sense of security.

"Once word got out that there was no one footing the bills, the construction crew that I was on just walked off the job. Two of them were coming home the week before I left." He thought of the one that had been killed at the airport, but decided not to mention that right now. "After that, it was a daily thing for someone to come looking for me to pay the bills. And they were high. Like tens of thousands of dollars each. Some of the materials that the project was being charged for were things that we didn't use and never would."

"Like what? I mean, as a builder, I understand that you'd know, but what sort of things?" He told him the few things that he'd seen on the bills. "Why would they need an in-ground pool? I mean, they're in the desert, for cripes sakes. And air conditioner units? Where did they think they were going to plug them in? These places that you're putting together, they're basically huts, correct?"

"Pretty much. We're not putting them in houses, because the first time we put a group of those up, the families were kicked out and some of the town leaders moved in. And it happened all over the place. So much so that the residents finally just stopped helping us and stayed away. I talked to a couple of them, ones that would talk to us anyway, and asked what they wanted. The hut was all they needed, they told me. A place to sleep without fear of being taken away in the night, and cool shade in the heat of the day."

"That is so sad. To only want a little shelter, and then have someone come along and try to make a profit from it. I'm sure that someone pointed out to these leaders they were hurting their own people, didn't they?" Brayden told his dad that it did little good. It was their country. "I suppose, but it still breaks my heart to think that the little we do is ruined like this."

"Is that why you came home? You quit your job there?"

He told his mom that was a part of it. "And the rest? Not this woman, I hope."

"In a way. She was asked to leave the country and not return. Something about a murder. I don't know all the details, as she won't tell me anything." Dad asked him what he thought might have happened. "She claimed it was self-defense. I have no way of knowing. But she had made a nuisance of herself and they wanted her gone. I heard just the other day that she had tried to make them sleep with her for money. Prostitution is not something that they turn a blind eye to there."

CHAPTER 4

Vonda sat on the bed and waited for Brady to come up and tell her he was sorry and that they were leaving. These people were going to ruin everything for her. It wasn't as if she hadn't told them that Brady belonged to her. Not outright, but she'd put some good hints out there. And then they did this to her. She was going to be their family too, wasn't she? What did they expect her to do, let them treat her badly? And Brady was no help at all. She thought he should have stood up for her, or slapped those people around at the very least. She knew that he'd come up soon, and she'd tell him they needed to leave now. This was no place for her to do what she wanted. And that was to get Brady to marry her.

They were trying to keep him from her, that was it. She knew that she shouldn't have ruined that old lady's flowers, but it was done and they should just get over it. And the fact that Vonda had slapped Brady had been a mistake to let them see. But then again, she had to show them that she was in charge. And as soon as they figured that out, including Brady, they'd be just fine.

He'd asked her to marry him, she knew that, but there was no ring yet. No date set, and she'd not been asked one thing about her plans for her big day. His mother had asked about the flowers, but they were second rate and would never do for what she had in mind for her big day. Why did that woman think she'd want flowers from her stupid garden anyway? It wasn't as if they didn't have the fucking money to make her day the best. She was really losing her temper with these people. They needed to get on the ball and make her happy, or else they'd never see their precious little boy again. Not that they didn't have five others to pamper too much.

Speaking of those other men…she hated them too. The brothers were not like Brady. Her soon-to-be husband was a pushover and controllable. Vonda had him right where she wanted him, and they had to open their big mouths. Christ, she'd be glad when she got her new home and would be able to bar them from her and Brady's life. It was going to be a great coup for her, to outwit the perfect Stantons.

Then there was the whole matter of a child. He was adamant about not wanting one. She wondered about that, but figured that a little slip up here or there would take care of that. And if he didn't want to cooperate on that score, she'd find someone that would. Perhaps one of the brothers would help her out. That way she could keep it all in the family. They might not care for her, but what man could turn down a woman like her? Well, Brady had, but that was soon to be taken care of too.

She might not like them, but they sure were a good-looking group of men. All of them, including the dad. Not that she'd sleep with him, but if it became an issue, then he'd do in a pinch. Vonda needed a child.

Not that she wanted one. No, children were messy, screaming things that needed entirely too much work for her to consider. But there were added benefits to having the children of a very rich man, and she was going to cash in on that. She might even let him visit them on occasion if he paid her enough. Vonda smiled. It really was all about the money.

She checked the little clock on the mantel over the fireplace and wondered what was taking him so long. They were more than likely holding him hostage or something. Keeping him away from her wouldn't work…they'd have to get over that soon too.

Vonda paced the spacious room. She wasn't going to go down without a fight either, she told herself. These people would have to learn that she would be ruling her home, and to fuck around with her would mean that they'd not see their son or brother, or any children of theirs when they came.

She paused in front of the window and looked out into the yard. The house was beautiful and the grounds were well maintained. She couldn't see the gardens from here, but had to smile when she thought of destroying those roses. Who cared that they were prized? They were just flowers. She liked the kind that Brady would pick up at the store for her more than she would some home-grown ones anyway. She'd have to get on him about that too. He'd never sent her any flowers or chocolate.

Her belly growled and she put her hand over it. She wondered if she called someone in the kitchen, if they'd bring her up something to eat. Going to the pulls at the window, she pulled on each of them, disappointed that they were just curtain ties. Didn't they have any way to ring for service in this place? She would have to make sure there was something she could use in her new home.

Even trying the phone, thinking that it would ring to someone down there, all she got for her effort was a dial tone. Vonda was even surprised that they had a landline. These people were so far behind in technology that she thought they'd not even have a computer or cable. That's when she realized that there was no television in the room.

51

"How the hell am I supposed to watch my shows now?" Vonda shook her head. "Where did these people come from? Under a rock?"

Resuming her pacing, she decided that her new home would have a television in every room. Maybe even the bathrooms as well. She was still smiling about that when she saw movement through the window she'd been looking out of earlier.

It was Brady. Where did he think he was going? As he made his way to the big pool area, she watched him as he opened the door to the nice sized house and stepped in. Waiting for several minutes, she realized that he was staying in there. As the lights in it were turned on then off a few minutes later, she stood staring at it in shock. What the fuck was he doing sleeping out there? She was never going to get a baby at this rate.

They'd never had sex...not for lack of trying on her part. Every time she would get him on the couch or in a closed-up room, she would throw herself at him, even going so far as to get down on her knees hoping to suck him off. It wasn't anything she enjoyed, but she needed him to fuck her. Vonda thought that a baby in the oven before the wedding would ensure that she'd not have to sign that stupid prenup, nor would he back out. Not that she was going to sign anything like that, but this would be her leverage. She also knew that any child of their life together, and even after their marriage ended, was going to be her savings account. But every time he would turn her down.

"Don't you like me?" He said that he did. She had waited for him to tell her that he loved her, but since she didn't love him, it was all right that he didn't say it. "I just want to show you how much I want you. I'm beginning to think you don't like sex or women. Is that it, Brady, you don't like women?"

"I love women. Very much so. And please stop calling me Brady." It pissed her off a little that he could love women in general, but only liked her. "But we're not married, and there is no point in rushing things."

She stared at him and then laughed. He had to be joking. There was no way that he'd just said that to her. When she asked him about it, he said that he was serious.

"You mean that you've never, not once in your single life, had sex outside of wedlock." He told her he had, but he'd never been engaged to anyone before. "Oh, so it's the fact that you're going to marry me that puts you off. I don't even have a ring yet, Brady. So, I guess technically we're not even engaged."

"I'm not going to sleep with you." She told him there wouldn't be much in the way of sleep. "It's not going to happen, Vonda. I want our wedding to be perfect, and sleeping with you beforehand would ruin that. And please, for the last time, will you stop calling me Brady."

After that, she called him that every time she spoke to him. She loved the way his eyes looked all mean and the vein in his forehead got larger. It was her pet name for him, and the fact that it ticked him off made it all the sexier to her. Vonda sat down on the bed and tried to think what she had to do now.

Since the first time she saw Brady, she knew that he was going to be perfect for her. Not just as her husband, but as her ex-husband as well. She didn't think they'd live happily ever after...that just didn't happen to people any more. Or at least she didn't think it did. It was what divorce was invented for. For people to get on with their lives a little better off than they were before marriage.

It wasn't as if she wanted to really marry, but he wasn't going to fork over the things she wanted without it. Like alimony and child support. She'd done a lot of research on the topic, and there was a lot to be gotten from the rich after a divorce, so long as she didn't sign the kind of paperwork he was shoving at her.

There was no way she was going to let him dictate what she got after she left him.

She looked around the big room and wondered if she should have asked which one she was going to use. This one was the biggest room she'd seen when she came up here, and the prettiest. It was as if they had decorated this room just for her. And she liked that when Brady came to see her, and he would, he'd have to go all the way down the hall to find her.

Vonda got up to look in the drawers to see whose room it might have been. As soon as she saw her own clothing in the drawers, she wondered why someone would do that. She'd not okayed someone touching her things. As she started to pull her clothing out of the drawers and toss it around the room, she realized that she'd been had, again. These people were going to have to get better at making her feel welcome. Because as of right now, she wasn't feeling anything but meanness. How dare they put her in a room so far from the rest of them?

At nearly midnight she went to bed. The room was a mess, but she wasn't going to bother with getting it neat again. That simply wasn't her job. Besides, she was pretty sure that they had servants for that sort of thing anyway. Why should she have to do their jobs? As she pulled the covers up to her chin, Vonda thought about the turn of events. Where had she lost control over Brady?

She wanted him to be upset with her on the plane when she'd left him there. The fact that he could easily sleep while she was sitting next to him had pissed her off. Going to find her own entertainment had been done to make him jealous. But he'd not said a single word. Not even to ask her about it when she told him what a good time she'd had. Something had changed in him, and she didn't care for it.

The house was too quiet as she lay there. She was used to

music everywhere she went. Brady would have known that if he had even once come to her apartment with her and slept over. But no, he had to be a prude. Vonda was going to start laying down the law soon. If he thought that she was going to put up with his moodiness, then he was going to be in big trouble. Rolling to her side, she thought of why she was marrying him.

Money. Plain and simple. He had it and she wanted it. But he was making her jump through hoops to get it and it was driving her insane. She wanted prestige too. As well as the status of his name, something that she'd be remembered by. Like, *oh look, there goes Vonda Stanton. I heard she married very well.* And she wanted people to notice her.

The lack of a ring on her finger bothered her a great deal. He'd had it in his head that someone would try and take it if he gave her one where they were. She supposed he was right in that. There were underlings all over the place where they'd been. She'd wanted him to stop at the jewelers on the way here from the airport, but his parents had said there wasn't time.

"Time? It'll only take a few hours. Surely you can carve that out of your day for your son to get his future wife a ring?" Brady had told her that now wasn't the time. "Brady, honey, it's the perfect time. You said when we got to the States. Well, here we are. And I think, after all you've put me through, I should have what I want."

Her requests went unanswered. And she was sure that his dad drove by each of the jewelry stores on purpose just to rub it in her face that she wasn't getting one today. Vonda needed to come up with a plan, one that would make Brady take her side against his overbearing family. Then he'd be hers, forever. Or until the divorce. Smiling, she closed her eyes. It was going to be a long day tomorrow…that was for sure.

~~~

55

Jane woke. It wasn't like she just opened her eyes and casually became alert like she normally did. It was sudden and scary. Reaching for her gun, she saw the man seconds before he spoke to her.

"I'm not going to harm you." The gun was too heavy in her hand and she was sure that it shook, but if she had to she'd fire first then figure it out later. "My name is Brayden Stanton. My dad is Denny...he's the doctor who treated you. I'm going to turn on the light so you can see me."

"I don't remember you." He said he'd only just arrived today. The light came on and she was blinded for a few seconds. She fully expected him to rush her, or at the very least take her gun, but when she looked where she'd heard him, he was sitting down on the chair. "You look like your father."

"Thank you. He's a good man. He told me that you were down here, and I thought I'd come and make sure you were all right." She was still sore, her body aching in the places that she knew from a conversation with Denny that she'd been hurt. "Are you?"

"I don't know. Am I?" He laughed and it made her feel fuzzy. "You said you were his son. How many does he have? I've met a few of them."

"Six. There are six of us, and I'm the oldest. Colton said you told him you weren't human and that he told you we were cougars." She said that was right. "Then you have some understanding of our kind? Like how we live?"

"I don't understand the question. You mean you don't live in a cave or something?" He laughed again, and told her what he meant. "Yes, I know about mates and children. I also know that purebloods, if that is what you are, can shift at any time after their first year. I have no idea how I remember that when I haven't any idea what my name is."

"We'll get to that. I'm here with someone." She looked around. "Not in here. She's upstairs. Hopefully asleep. I came home to get married to her, but now I can't. She's not a nice person anyway, and my family hates her. Not that I blame them. I don't care much for her either."

"Then why did you ask her to marry you if she's not nice? I'd have thought that would have been a deal breaker from the get go." He said he thought so as well. "Why are you really down here? I'm pretty sure that with it being as late as it is, you could have just waited until morning."

"You're my mate. I figured it out when I came down here with my dad earlier tonight. You were resting, but I knew." Jane said nothing. "I don't know what to do. I mean, I have a few ideas, but I'd rather not end up in prison before you and I can have a nice long life together. If you're willing to, that is."

"I don't know what you should do either. But as for a long life, not going to happen even if you didn't have a fiancée hanging around. I would say that it sucks to be you, but that doesn't seem like a nice thing to say. I don't want to be lumped in with the woman you are marrying." He nodded, then shook his head. "You're very strange. Has anyone told you that before?"

"Not to my face, no. But I really am in trouble here. This woman, Vonda, I think she's played me for a fool." It was on the tip of her tongue to tell him that he was one if he was marrying a woman he didn't like. "She was all gooey and easy when we were in Africa, and now she's like this bitch from hell. She even murdered my mom's roses. Mom loves her flowers, and she just stomped them in the ground."

"Sounds like a good reason to me not to marry her. Murdering flowers is a no-no." He looked at her, confused, and she laughed. "I'm kidding. I don't know your mom well enough to know if she's upset about her flowers being destroyed. But even so, that was a pretty shitty thing to do. Once when I was younger, the neighbor cut down my father's favorite holly bush. It was there when we left for the day and...I just had a memory."

"Finish it." She nodded, then shook her head. "Is it gone or you're not going to tell me about it? I'm interested to know what your father did about it."

"When we returned from shopping—Christmas shopping, I think—the bush was strewn all over the yard. Even the lights—there were green and red lights in it—they were smashed up and lying over the hacked-up branches." She laid back on the bed and closed her eyes, letting the memory finish. "He picked up the branches and took them in the house. He wasn't one to get angry, but I knew that he was. So, he makes this beautiful wreath out of them. It was the most gorgeous thing I had ever seen. He dug out some more lights and wrapped them around it. There were balls of red and green too. And a large velvet bow that he hung on the top. And when he was finished, he took it to the neighbor's house and stuck it on his front door."

"That was nice. Did you ever find out why he'd done it?" She nodded and felt her head hurt again. "Don't force it. Colton said that when you remember something, you should tell someone whatever it is. It makes it more real."

"His name was Scrimshaw. He was.... I don't remember what he did or where this happened, but his name I can." Brayden said that was good. "He was upset because my father had decorated the house for the holidays the weekend after Thanksgiving. He thought that he should have waited for an entire week before doing so. For some reason, he thought that destroying the bush and lights would make my father see his side."

Her head was pounding again, but she didn't use the drugs that were readily available to her. She wanted to talk to this man. Not get to know him, but just talk. He seemed like he was as lonely as she was. And when he stood up and moved the chair and himself closer to the bed, she realized he was a very big man. Not fat, but big. She figured that he was at least six and a half feet tall, and weighed between two-thirty and two-fifty. He was muscled and good looking, with blondish golden hair that was just long enough to touch his shoulders if it wasn't curling up like it was. His green eyes made her think of the cat that he was, and he had perfect white teeth that she could imagine him biting into her with.

"You're not making this any easier on me." She stared at him. "You're beautiful. And I can smell you. You're aroused."

"So? It doesn't mean anything. You're taken, in case you forgot that." He nodded and looked so sad that she wanted to take back her mean comment. "Look, you need to go away before she comes down here and finds you with me. I'm sure, from your description of her, she'll not take kindly to you being with another woman. Even if it is innocent."

"You're probably right. She thinks that I'm going to give her whatever she wants. Even a big house, and a child." She asked him if she was his mate too. "No. I was...I don't want to say settling, but that's basically what I was doing. I was lonely and for a time, she filled the void. But almost as soon as I proposed, she became this nightmare of a person. Demanding and telling me.... She calls me Brady. I hate it."

"Have you told her not to call you that?" He told her several times. "Then she needs to have her ass handed to her. I can't stand people like that. I don't think I can anyway. I believe there is more going on here than I can remember. I mean, little things like my dad's bush and lights aren't going to tell me much more than I had a good man as a father."

He laughed. Not a little one, but the full belly kind that made her smile. He was funny when he let himself be, and she liked that he could laugh at himself. But he had issues that were bigger than a few laughs with a stranger.

"May I hold your hand?" She said it was okay with her so long as that was all he did. "I'd very much like to do more, but I know that you're hurt and we don't know each other that well."

"I don't even know me that well. For all you know, I could have a husband and five kids right now." Brayden told her she didn't have any children nor a husband. "And how the hell do you know that?"

"You're a virgin." That wasn't what she expected him to say. "Would you like to know what else I have observed about you?"

"Yes, but if you think this is going to get you laid, you'd better rethink that. Obviously I don't put out, so you'd better be careful. And I have a gun too. While I don't know anything about my former life, I do think I can use it without problems." He promised that he would be careful with her from now on. There was something about the wording that threw her, but she told him to go on.

"You're very comfortable with that gun, as you said. You didn't hesitate to pull it out when you thought you were in danger, but you didn't shoot anyone that was trying to help you...my brother first, then my dad when you woke. While you allowed me to be in the room with you, you would have been ready to not just wound me, but kill me if you needed to. And even now, you have the gun at the ready even though you sort of trust that I won't harm you." All true, she told him. He asked to take her hand in his. "You're also proficient with a knife. I would say that you might carry one, but it's not a girly kind but a switchblade. You cut yourself on it a lot in the beginning, but not anymore."

She thought about a knife. "I have a black one with a matte shell. The blade is long and sharp and I keep it clean. I wear it in my boot. Right one, deep in the inside of it." He got up to get her boot and dumped it on the bed. The knife was just as she had described. "What does that mean?"

"I don't know. But so far, you've had two memories while I've been in here, and I would call that progress. Shall I continue?" She told him to please go ahead. "Dad said you had no identification on you, which makes me think you were robbed or you don't wear it when you're working. Robbery doesn't ring right because you are still armed, and no one took that from you. I think you were working, because you were armed well and shot. I also don't think you're a bad guy in this scenario, but maybe a cop or something undercover."

Jane told him she didn't know, but she didn't feel like she was a bad person. He nodded and turned her hand over. The IV was there, just below her middle finger, but it was the mark on her hand that he was examining. It was a through and through kind of scar. She asked him if he knew what it was.

"I think so. It looks like you've been hit with a nail gun. Like the kind that has power to it and is used in putting together houses." She asked him if he was a construction worker. "In a way. But the reason I know this mark is because one of the men that I was working with recently hit his hand with a gun like the one I was describing."

"Did he do it on purpose?" Brayden told her that he was trying to impress a woman. "What an idiot. I don't suppose it occurred to him that it wasn't something that women usually go for? I mean, Christ, he blew a hole in his hand, and I bet that

61

she didn't even go visit him in the hospital, did she?"

"There wasn't a hospital. So a few days after he did that, he got an infection. It killed him. There aren't a lot of medical facilities where I was, either." He put her hand back on the bed and looked at her. "I'm sorry. I have no idea why I told you that story. I guess I'm really screwing up here."

"No. I mean, it wasn't a pick me up, but it was a story. But I'm glad that you shared it with me. You were somewhere bad, I take it." He told her where he'd been and for how long. "So, you were there to build houses then? For the people there?"

"They were more like huts, but yes. I volunteer a few times a year. This time I stayed far too long because of the problems I ran into. Almost six months. But before that, I was gone for nearly two years. I used to travel a great deal. That's where I met Vonda. Her father was one of the people trying to gather money for us to use. But something happened with that too, and he sort of disappeared a few months ago...his wife as well. I never thought to consider it, but I've since talked to a couple of people, so who knows where that'll go. I started out just having an occasional dinner with Vonda. Then I realized... well, I realized too late that I wasn't with the right person." Jane nodded. "I really messed up all our lives by jumping the gun, so to speak. Where did you live with your father?"

"Washington, DC." She looked at him and smiled. "Your brother does that too. Colton. He catches me off guard then asks a question. It's tricky, but it works."

He nodded. "It's not much, but every little clue can help us find out where you're from. No one is looking you up on the computer, by the way. My brother Julian was a police officer for a little while, and he said that if anyone is looking for you, that would be the way that they'd find you." She asked him why he wasn't a cop now. "He was shot in the line of duty. Which wouldn't have been so bad, but someone saw him shift to heal. His boss told him he'd be better off taking an early retirement, because after that no one wanted to work with him. Which really sucks. Julian was really good at his job. But he enjoys what he does now."

"Which is what?" He told her he was a private investigator. Something tingled along her skin and Brayden took her hand in his. "Did that bother you? Something about him being a PI?"

"I don't know. Something...I just don't know, and when I think too hard, my head pounds." He nodded. "I'm really tired now. If you'll just go, I'll be fine now."

"I'd like to sit with you for a little while. Just...I don't want to go back out to the pool house. I won't bother you."

She nodded, her head making her sick. As she pressed the button to give her some relief, she heard him say something about Nelson Pharmaceuticals. It was too late for her to say anything about it, but she felt fear all the way to her toes.

CHAPTER 5

Brayden watched her sleep until the sun rising started to fill the room with light. He wasn't bored, but he was in awe of her. While she'd been sleeping, he'd done some poking around with his dad's computer. Not about her, but about the venture that he'd been on before coming home.

The housing project, one that he'd been involved in for over a decade, was falling apart around their ears. He was glad now that he'd left when he had. Investigations were going on now that were going to put a lot of people in jail. Donations had been waylaid and not paid to the people who were providing supplies at a very big discount. And the things that had been donated—food, water, and such—were gone too. No one, it seemed, knew where or when they had disappeared.

The article was saying that nearly fifty million in donations were gone, and about that much more in tangible donations such as blankets, medical kits, and clothing. He would hate to be on that end of the investigation. But he had a feeling at some point in this, he was going to have to go back and testify.

After he had found all he wanted, he looked for the article about Vonda. Brayden had told his family all that he knew. Which to be honest, wasn't a great deal. He thought, now that he was home, her being asked to leave the country after finding the man's body had been what had made him realize that he couldn't go through with the marriage. Even if he hadn't met his mate here, he would have had to break it off. She was too... Vonda was insane. And he was sure he wasn't overthinking that. Vonda destroying the roses for no other reason than they were there made him think she was vindictive as well. Then there was the thing with her not listening. He was sure she was getting what he was telling her about children, but since she didn't like his answers, she simply ignored it. Much like she did with him telling her repeatedly not to call him Brady. There was a screw or two loose there somewhere.

When the two of them had made their way to the airport that morning to leave to come here, it had been hectic. His plan had been to leave her there, go home, then come back for her. But she wanted to go and he just didn't want to listen to her any longer, so he agreed to take her with him. After that was when she started to become what he could only assume now was her true self.

The police were waiting for them at the airport. He was confused, thinking that he was being brought in for something at the site. But when they asked to speak to Vonda, she told them it was self-defense. Just like that, without them asking any questions. Brayden felt his cat curl around him when he heard her telling the police what had happened.

"He came up behind me and jerked me around. I was cutting up some bread for a sandwich when he did that, and I lashed out with the knife." Brayden knew that wasn't true. He knew this woman and she never cut up bread, nor did she make herself food when there were restaurants or other people around to do it for her. "When I saw what I'd done, I panicked and called Brady."

The officer looked at him. He wasn't going to lie for her, and told them she'd not called him. But she insisted and he had to take out his phone and show them that he'd not gotten any calls from her. Then they asked to see hers.

"I don't know where it is. I might have left it at my house in the panic. I know now that I should have called someone, but like I said, he scared me. And I did call Brady. I spoke to him twice about what I had done." Again, he denied talking to her and asked them to pull his phone records or hers. But her anger surged forward and he had backed away from her with it. "You will not. I have things on my phone records that I don't want you to see. Brady, just tell them you and I talked and we'll be on our way home. We're getting married when we get to his parents' lovely home."

From then on, he had had enough. He told them several times that he'd never spoken to her, and agreed to sign what they needed to pull his phone records to check. She was angry at him before they boarded the plane, and it wasn't until they were in the air that she acted as if nothing had happened.

The long plane ride had only made it worse. The police said that they'd be in touch and took his information. When Vonda refused to give them hers, he told them to call him and he'd make sure to tell her. There was no way he was going to end up in prison for her. And when he'd tried to talk to her about it on the ride here, she told him it was too depressing to talk about and wouldn't say a word. It had been the beginning of the end of any kind of relationship for them.

He found two articles about the incident. The first one said that Martin Millner had been killed at an undisclosed location and they were investigating it. There was little said in the first article, and neither he nor Vonda were mentioned, but the second one said a great deal.

Millner had been staying at the large hotel in town, apparently. And Vonda Hull and he had been having a pugnacious affair. On again and off again, the two of them had fights so loudly that the neighboring clientele would call in the police weekly to get them to shut up. Brayden read more of the article on how Vonda had been brought in for questioning once when Millner had been injured so badly that he'd needed a hospital stay. She had said they were having a tiff and that he'd fallen down the stairs. Millner had claimed that she'd pushed him. Of course, she had denied it.

The rest of the article talked about Millner, and how he'd been in trouble with the law himself. Robbery for one. Drugs another time. It seemed to Brayden that the two of them were more suited than she and Brayden were. Then he got to the last part of the article.

"Vonda Hull is wanted for questioning in the murder of Mr. Millner. She and her companion have fled to the United States, and we're working to have her returned at this time. There are discrepancies in her statement to the police, and we would ask that if you have any information on the death of Mr. Millner or Miss Hull's disappearance to please call our office."

Brayden closed the computer and sat there. He wondered why they'd not called him. He'd given them all the information that they needed to contact either of them, including his parents' home line. He pulled out his phone and found that someone had blocked the number that he knew was from that area. Vonda had somehow gotten his phone and done that, he knew it.

The sun was fully up now, and he could hear his family was beginning to stir on the upper floors. When his dad showed up about half an hour later, Brayden was still sitting at his desk thinking. He was in a great deal of trouble here and wasn't sure how to fix it.

"Son?" He nodded at his dad but said nothing. He was still

trying to process what he'd just read and figured out. "Have you been here all night?"

"Yes. I wanted to come and talk to her. She's my mate." Dad sat down but didn't comment. Brayden wasn't sure what he was thinking, but he continued before he could ask him anything. "I thought so when you and I came down here yesterday, then I came in to talk to her later, and she is. I don't know what we're going to do, but for now she has to heal and I have to get rid of Vonda. I just found out a couple of things. I might be in a little trouble here with her."

"What sort of trouble?" He told his dad everything. Showed him his phone and the article that he'd just read. "They don't mention your name. You think that's an oversight or that they don't think you're involved?"

"I don't know that either. I know that they have it...my name, I mean. What I don't understand, if it was like she said, is why she'd avoid the calls and go to such lengths to keep from talking to them. This only makes her sound guiltier." His dad agreed with him. "Dad, I think I need to contact them and get this mess taken care of. This woman is my mate, and I can't have this going on with Vonda."

"Yes. That sounds like a good plan." Dad looked over at the woman then back at him. "I have to tell you something then. I don't know rightly what I'm going to do about it, but you should know. I took a bullet out of her leg. It was a tracker as best I can tell."

"Tracker? How do you know?" He described it to him. "What would she be doing with that in her leg? And where is it now? We don't want anyone coming here for her, not without knowing anything about her."

"I put it in the autoclave machine. It's all metal and thick, so I figured no one could get it to work in that. I didn't destroy it though, which was my first thought, but kept it. It might be something we need at some point. When she gets her full memories back perhaps she can tell us what it's for." Dad looked at the woman again. "I'm not sure what Nelson Pharmaceuticals has to do with her, but she's mentioned them a couple of times. Do you think she worked there and figured something out?"

"I don't know. I mean, what could she have found out from them that would get her killed?" Dad told him there were all kinds of reasons that came to mind. "Yes, I would imagine that you'd have better insight on this than me. But I don't know. What else? I think you're not telling me something. What is it?"

"She has a mark on her back. I thought at first it was something to do with a group of beings that I heard of as a kid, but when I took a good look at it and searched for it in one of your grandmother's old books, I found that it was different. I don't have any idea why she's marked that way." His dad pulled out his phone and showed him the picture he'd taken of it and of the one that had been in the book. "They're nearly the same, but as you can see, there are minor shifts in the drawing. Where the one in the book is round, hers is oval. Also, there are no colors on hers. And I looked at it hard...it's not a tattoo, but a burn. The scarring is old, at least a decade or two, and it's been taken care of. Like someone didn't want her to be sick from it."

"What does it mean? I mean the one in the book? What does the book say this mark means, and where did it come from originally?" His dad got up and pulled an old book from his shelves. He would never have seen it had he been searching for it. There were a great many older books in this part of the house. His dad loved to read, and he would read just about anything that was in print.

Brayden read the pages that his dad marked while he

70

checked on the woman. He was going to have to figure out a name for her. "That woman" was just too callous sounding. Brayden looked up when he'd finished reading.

"It says that the tribe would mark a woman this way when they found that she was an adulteress. Even if she had been raped, they'd blame her for it and then mark her on the face like this. As barbaric as it sounds, not much has changed from some of the things I've seen while I've been traveling." Dad said he knew that as well. "So, what does this have to do with Nelson if anything, and why has she been burned with this thing on her back?"

"Only she can answer that, I think." Dad sat back down. "I've not told your mom nor the others about the tracker. And she and I are the only ones that know about the mark, too. I don't know why, but I have a feeling that if too many people were aware of not only those things but her being here as well, we'd be in a heap of trouble, son."

"I think you're right. I don't know why, but I have a feeling that you are completely right on all of it." As they made their way up the stairs, Brayden wondered what he was going to do about Vonda. First and foremost, he had to ask her about being pursued by the police from where she'd killed a man.

~~~

Brayden was back again. This time he was resting in the chair with his feet up on the big desk. Jane watched him sleep and wondered where Vonda was. He had told her that she was clingy last night, and she wondered if he'd sent her back. It would have been the smart thing to do, but not for her. The man wasn't happy. When he stretched, she could see that he was a well-built man, not an ounce of fat anywhere on him. When he came to her bed, she looked up at him and was amazed at the color of his eyes.

71

"I thought that cougars had golden eyes. Yours are green." He smiled and sat down after pulling the chair over. "You must have someone human in your line, right?"

"No, actually. We're purebloods and can trace our history back for generations. I'm not saying that it's not possible, I suppose, but my mom's eyes are green too. I think it's a dormant trait that she and I share." He took her hand in his. "How are you today? Feeling any better? And by the way, that's three memories for you now."

"I have no trouble with facts, its personal things that I don't know. Like who or what I am. And when I think about it, I get this pain in my head that makes me sick enough to want to puke on you. Have you been looking for answers?" He said that he could only smell her as a human. "So, I might not be something else."

"Not necessarily. I mean, whatever you are—and it could still only be human—you could also have something that hides you from others." She felt a twinge of a memory, but it was there and gone too fast for her to catch. "Don't force them. They'll come to you the more you heal. Colton said for you to just talk about whatever you want, and something might trigger them."

"I have something that I can't think around. It's a lab of sorts. Nelson Pharmaceuticals. Every time I think of it, or someone mentions it, I feel a fear that is crippling." She looked at the wall in front of her and not Brayden. "It's like when you're hurt or sick. Whatever happened or ate, that memory stays with you forever. So, when you're offered say, pizza again, the memory of it makes your belly sick. That's the way I feel when I think of Nelson."

"Just fear with it, or sick too?" She said that it was both. Then she looked at him when he continued. "You have a mark on your back. My dad found it and told me about it this morning. What do you remember about it, if anything?"

"I'm to be destroyed." She closed her eyes at the things that memory brought to her. "A man was going to put a bullet in my head. I can see him as clear as day. His face is set and he looks like he's on some kind of drugs. It's making him mindless to his own thoughts. He pulls out the gun and aims at me. Someone there is begging. I can't tell for what, but they're crying. But I'm not going down easy. I must save myself. So, I lunge and...I think I killed him by breaking his neck."

The memory washed over her. The man was dead, yet she held his body in front of her as a shield and killed the two men there with them. His gun was the one that was at her hip now. It was hers, he'd taken it from her to kill her with it. The other men, two of them she remembered now, fell forward as she shot out a window to escape. It stopped right there, just as she was running out of the building.

"Do you think that was when you were shot?" Jane told him she didn't think so but wasn't sure. "What did the building look like? Did you glance back? Was there anything in the room that you can make out?"

"It was sterile. I'm not sure why I think that...perhaps it was because the walls were white. The two men were in coats, but not white like the walls. They were...blue." He asked her if they were coats or suits. "Yes. That's it. They were covered in this blue thing. So was their hair but not their faces. They wore masks over them for...I think to not smell something."

"I don't know where this is, but it helps. It could very well be in Nelson, but since I've never been in the building, I have no way of knowing for sure. But if they're a pharmaceutical company, why are they trying to kill people? I haven't any idea, do you?" She asked him if he had heard what she said about killing those men. "Yes. You saved yourself. There is no other way to see it. You were going to be killed and you did what you needed to."

"But what if I had done something wrong that warranted it?" He asked her if she was in a courtroom or a lab. "Lab. Oh, I see where you're going. So, they were killing me for something that I did there. Had I been on trial or something, then there would have been a courtroom and a judge. Are you a detective?"

"No, just a man. However, the papers call me a philanthropist. Or a humanitarian. Any name you want to call a man who has nothing better to do than give away money and his free time, that'd be me." He grinned and looked so boyish that she smiled back at him. "I invented a couple of things when I was younger and sold the plans to a big company. Not really invented so much as I found a way to improve on a machine that was already in use. It's what I excel in, I guess you could say. And since then, I've been making other things that are worth a great deal to people. You might call me an inventor, but I just say I'm a man who likes to make things easier on people."

He told her of the project that he'd been working on, as well as the trouble that had brewed up with it. She didn't have anything to add to it; and no idea what she could have said anyway. Brayden was a wealthy man, and she was.... Well, nothing as far as she knew.

"Vonda still here?" He told her she was, sadly. "What are you going to do about her? I'm not saying that you should get rid of her because of me, but you must do something. She sounds unbalanced. What if she goes ape shit or something and you have to hurt her to calm her? That's going to look bad on all of you, don't you think?"

"I think you're right." He told her about the man and the article that he'd read. "So, my thinking is that she's taken my phone at some point and had the calls redirected. I don't know about my parents' line. I've not heard anything from the staff about it. At some point, I think, they're going to call looking for her. I've talked to my family, and they're not going to cover for her either. She has to be made to realize that we're finished."

"Good luck with that. Like I said, she's off her noodle. Who does that to someone they're supposed to marry? And to your mom? She brought me soup last night. She said she made it." He told her his mom was a great cook. "And nice. I like her."

Jane didn't know a great deal about the rich, or if she did she didn't remember it, but she doubted very much that they cooked for strangers. And did such a great job at it. He told her about himself.

He'd graduated from college a little young, being seventeen when he'd gotten out. He and his brothers were all professionals, each of them out of college and on their own now. Grinning, he told her about his parents and how they had come to make them want to be successful.

"My parents never gave us anything that we didn't either need or earn. Some people think that we were given everything on a silver platter, when that couldn't be further from the truth. When I got my first new car, it was because I had worked hard to get it. I even paid my own insurance, as well as my car payments. The same with the rest of us." She asked him if he had a house. "No. I've been traveling for a while now and I've never settled down. I'm currently looking for us a home. What did you have in mind for one?"

"You can't think I'm going to live with you." He nodded and frowned. "You know nothing about me. For all you know I could have a death warrant over my head and someone is out to kill me. Which I'm pretty sure is what is going on."

"I don't care. I mean, I do, but I'll help you." She shook her head. "You're my mate. Speaking of which, what should I call you? I mean, do you have a name that you like?"

"Dane." She had no idea why that had popped into her head, but once it was there, memories came flooding back. "My name is Dane Mueller. Oh, Brayden. I'm Dane Mueller. I have no family, nor do I have a house. I live off the streets. I don't know why, but I think I have money."

"That's wonderful. I'm so very glad to meet you, Dane Mueller." He kissed her then, a quick touching of the lips, then he looked down at her and leaned in again. This time it was a kiss meant to curl toes and make a body hum. When he sat back down, neither of them said anything for several moments. She was trying to figure out some of the things that were racing in her mind. He just looked confused.

"I should tell you that while I remember a great deal, I'm not married." He looked at her and laughed. "Are you all right? I mean, it wasn't that horrific, was it?"

"No. I mean it was wonderful. But you're not human. I mean, you don't taste human." His face turned a nice shade of pink. "What I meant was, I know that you're not wholly human, but I'm not sure what you are either."

"You can taste that I'm not human?" He nodded and took her hand to his mouth and kissed it. "What would you have to do to figure that out? I mean, you could, right?"

"Yes, I could bite you." He looked at her throat and she felt her body warm up. "I would love to taste all of you. And then eat you, but you're still not on the healthy side just yet. And I need to deal with Vonda."

Vonda. The woman was becoming a pain in the ass and she'd not even met her. Dane had a feeling that if or when she did, it wasn't going to be pretty. The woman was going to have to get the hell out of here and leave them alone. It was something she was going to work on as soon as she figured out how.

Dane looked around the room when Brayden was called away. She wanted to get up and move around, but she didn't want to hurt herself and be in bed longer. Instead, she thought of the memories that she now had. Like the last thing she remembered and how she'd ended up here.

Nelson was the root of all the problems she was having. The day that she had escaped wasn't the day she was nearly killed. Dane had escaped months prior…she knew that now. She had been in the compound before she was hurt that day, but this time not as a guest.

One of the big bay doors that the trucks used to bring in merchandise had provided her with easy entry. Why she had been there still eluded her, but she was armed and ready to defend…. Whatever she'd been there to do, it wasn't to visit or to get a refill on her prescriptions. Someone needed her. They wanted her to get them out. It was a promise she'd given that person.

As the memories made themselves known to her, her head hurt, but not like before. There was something more, something she was missing that she needed to remember. What it had been was what had caused her to be hurt.

Names popped into her head. David and a man named Davie. Peter, who she remembered was Nelson, the owner of the pharmaceutical company. There was a man named Damian as well. This man, she knew, had been the one that had ordered her death, but the reason behind it was still not coming. As she lay there, sorting what she knew and didn't know, things became clearer to her. Memories were starting to go in a nice straight line. One led right back to Nelson. Then it hit her. She knew now.

Dr. Stanton came down about an hour later. He asked her if she was all right and handed her a towel. When she wiped at her nose as he had suggested, she saw the blood. Looking at him, she saw concern and fear.

"Brayden said that you had some memories come to you." She nodded. "You remembered your name. That's good, right? I'm betting there is more too, isn't there?"

"Yes, but I don't know if sharing them is a good idea just yet." She didn't want to tell him what else she remembered, but wiped at her nose again. "Some of them are hard to believe are real. It's like I'm seeing me differently than the way that I feel."

"Understandable. You've been hurt and you're not sure why. Then you wake up here, and while you're remembering things, you're still lost." He took her blood pressure as well as her temperature. "I was thinking to let you up and about today. Do you think you can handle sitting in a chair for a little while?"

"Oh yes, please. I know that I can't go upstairs yet, not with Vonda there, but I would love to sit by the window and feel the sunshine on my face." He said that he could let her do that, but did caution her to be careful. "I will."

Getting her to the wheelchair was easy. Dane knew that paranormals were strong, but she also knew that she wasn't a lightweight. But Denny, as he insisted she call him, picked her up and set her into the chair with ease. Her body felt exhausted after the move, and she'd not even done anything. She wondered how long it would be before she was recovered from this.

"It's the loss of blood, as well as the fact that you've not been eating much. I'll have Lucy bring you something a little more substantial for lunch later." She thanked him as he moved her over to the door that led to the backyard. He told her there was a deck overhead that they used a great deal in the summer, but no one was out there now. "By the way, Brayden has left for a little while. He and his brothers are running an errand for their mom. Should be back just after lunch. Vonda is here but she's in a funk, I'm to understand. Her and Brayden had a tiff." He laughed.

"I'm thinking it was more than a tiff." With a laugh, he said it was a ripper. "I see. Anything that I might enjoy hearing about?"

"Oh, I just bet you would. You see, she's been avoiding calls from the police where her and my son were. Brayden said that if she didn't speak to them before he got back, he was going to call them on her behalf. She seems to think he's being a bit mean to her. I would have hit her...actually, I'm the gentlemanly type and wouldn't, but she sure does tempt a man. I have to tell you, I'm very happy that he's found you as a mate. He wouldn't have married this other woman anyway, not after all she's done. And you're going to be getting up and around soon, I think. We'll just have to make sure that you don't overdo things for now."

When he left her, saying he had some things to do for his wife, he gave her his spare cell phone. He told her that when they went out to dinner, he and his wife, he had the spare in the event that the hospital needed him. It was annoying, he said, that people would call for no other reason than they thought he needed whatever they were selling. She supposed that if it were his family, they'd not need something so mundane as a phone.

It occurred to her then that she'd had a phone, and wondered what had become of it. And how she might figure out where it was. There were things on it, she knew, that would get her killed. Also, she had a feeling that it wasn't in the hands of Peter or Damian.

CHAPTER 6

Brayden listened to the detective, Patrick Helm, on the other end of his phone as he took notes. The police there had it in their head that Vonda had killed Millner, and that it wasn't self-defense as she'd told them. Brayden didn't agree nor disagree with them, but he needed more information. The police had a great deal of proof that Millner wasn't her only victim in this rampage she'd gone on before leaving with him. Brayden now had a list of missing and presumed dead people all over the area he'd been working. Two of them were a part of the group he'd been working with while there.

"You're sure you know it was her? Not that I doubt you, but are you sure?" Patrick told him some of the things they'd found at not just her place, but another home where they'd found a body. "Christ. I had no idea. What is it you want me to do? Tell me and you'll have it."

"First of all, we need to have her back here. We could come and get her, but that is not going to bode well for her if we do. If you can convince her that she needs to atone for her crimes, we can work some sort of deal out with her." He wasn't sure how that was going to work and told him so. "Yes, we've heard from a couple of people about her temper. I'm sorry, Dr. Stanton, for your involvement in this, but she's left us no choice."

"I understand. And please, call me Brayden. I have a

doctorate, but I rarely use it as a title." Patrick said he could do that as he laughed, and said if he had one, he'd be writing it on everything. Brayden laughed with him. "I can't get her to call your offices. I've tried everything. She claims that you're setting her up to take the fall for this. I'm not sure now what the fall might be that she's talking about. She has a lot of questions to answer, if you ask me. That's why I've made this call to you. I've told her if she didn't call by this evening I was going to do it for her, but I wanted to talk to someone first. I was thinking to see what it is she's being questioned for."

"Millner was killed three days before you left here as best we can tell. Then as we were searching the apartment that they were sharing, we found other things. Pictures of victims, bloodied clothing, as well as gloves that were in plastic bags with names on them. Once we started looking into those names, it led us to more bodies and more evidence. And not only were Millner's prints on things, but the majority of the items had hers on them as well. It's a mess here. A terrible mess."

He told him he was sorry again, that he'd do what he could. The man put him on hold as someone entered his office. As Brayden waited for him to come back on the line, his brother Levi entered his office. He'd started telling him what they'd found when Patrick came back on the line.

"Brayden, have you seen her father lately? I mean, when you were here, did you speak to or have any contact with her father?" He said that he'd been under the impression that he was traveling a great deal, that he'd only met him the one time, at a fundraiser some months ago. "We think we've found him. He and his wife, they're both deceased if it's them. We're running tests now, but I'm sure it's going to come back as her parents."

"Good Christ. I had no idea." Patrick told him they hadn't

either until they brought in a search team and dog. "She'll be back there, even if I have to tie her up and bring her to you."

"That won't be necessary now. We'll come for her. The number of bodies we have that she may be responsible for is too high for us to assume that she's going to come easily. No. If you'd be so kind as to not mention this to her, we'll be there in two days." Brayden said he'd do that. "Good. Thank you for your cooperation, Brayden. I'm not sure what we would have done had you not called. This is a royal mess, and I'll be glad to see the end of it."

Not as much as he would, Brayden thought. He wanted to get on with his life. Give his new mate a home. He didn't even care if she ever got her memory back. He was sure that she would, with the memories that she was getting now, but he was enjoying being with her.

He told Levi most of what he'd been able to find out, even the part about Dane being his mate. Understandably, Levi was worried. Brayden was as well. Not so much about what would happen with Vonda, but what she was going to do once they came for her. Murder was a big deal in every country, but the death of so many was just too horrific for words.

"If I were you, I'd avoid her altogether. I mean, not even to sit near her at the table. She'll be pissy about it, but we'll be there to help. I've got some things going right now, but nothing that can't wait until she's gone." Brayden thanked him. "No problem with that, big brother. We're all here for you. And if she gets too much out of line, they'll never find her body. That you can take to the bank."

"I'm afraid. Not of her, but of what sort of mess she can cause here." Levi said that he needed to tell everyone what Dane was to him. "I will tonight at dinner. Vonda told Mom that she's not eating with the family any more. She claims we're

83

all out to make her feel bad. Mom just told her to shut up and left her in the bed. This was at noon, mind you. Dad told me Dane is up and about too."

He had been enjoying talking to her about his days, playing chess, and reading. They'd not once had an argument. Never had either of them spoken harshly to the other. It was a nice, comfortable beginning, and Brayden loved it. Also for the fact that she'd not once called him Brady, a name that he was beginning to detest.

"So now what happens?" Levi listened as he told him what Patrick had said that they were going to do. "So, they think she killed her own parents? What a horrific person. I'm glad that you're going to break it off with her, Brayden. She scares the crap out of me the way she sits and stares at you without saying a word. And Mom showed me the garden this morning. Apparently, she's been out there again. She broke all the bushes but one, and it was the white one behind the garage for the extra sun. Christ, what a fucking bitch."

"I know. I told Mom that I'd take care of it for her, and she told me she needed to plan first. I think she wants to start over with some new things. Levi, I just want this done. And to be able to let Dane out of the basement. She's been sort of hiding there so that Vonda doesn't see her. There is no telling what she might do if she found out about Dane being my mate." Levi said he thought that Dane could hold her own. Brayden laughed. "Maybe you're right. I never thought of that. Maybe we should put them in a room together and let them have at it. Might save us all some time, don't you think?"

"Mom and Dad will have to know." He said that he'd tell them later. "Good. If you don't mind, I'll let the others know. I think they're ready to run out anyway. Julian said he had to get back to work, and I know that Colton went to his offices yesterday. You might be the only ones here if she keeps this up."

"I'm going to talk to Dane tonight. Did you hear that Christian found something about her in the paper?" He said that he had heard. "I don't know what to think about it. I mean, for all we know it could be the same people that hurt her that are now looking for her. Putting a missing person article in the paper seems sort of scary at this point, don't you think? But it sounds like this guy really wants to find her."

"That's what Christian said. He even talked to the guy this morning. His name is Davie James. Christian said that he was talking to another client or something, and that his name had come up about a missing person. I guess Christian asked him if he needed anyone to help out." Brayden had heard that the man had sobbed that he was missing Dane and wanted her to come back home. "From what he's been able to find out, Dane is no relation to him but they hung out together when she wasn't working. And before you ask, no, he has no idea what she does for a living, but he knows that on occasion she is hurt."

No one knew but him and his dad that Dane was remembering more all the time. Just that morning she'd told him where the gun had come from. He wasn't worried about that so much as he was that she would remember something so horrific that she'd be devastated. Tonight they were going to talk about the newspaper article and what this man Davie meant to her. If she could remember. Brayden had a feeling that she not only remembered the name, but she might have already figured out a lot of other stuff as well.

~~~

Dane, using the cane that Denny had given her, made her way back to bed. She was getting stronger every day, but she still wasn't all that steady on her feet yet. Dane was nearly to the bed when the door opened and Brayden said it was him from the other room. She relaxed then, holding onto the bed until he came in. She smiled when she smelled the Chinese food he had in big bags.

"I thought we'd have a treat. Dad said it would be all right if we did. Vonda is resting. She didn't sleep well last night, she said." Dane knew why she hadn't. She'd seen her in the yard at about three this morning tearing up the garden. The woman was going to be treading on thin ice if she ever got the pleasure of seeing her face to face. "You said you liked dumplings and fried rice, so I got a variety of other things to have with it. I hope you don't mind."

They were opening the small containers when his hand brushed over hers. It was getting harder and harder to ignore the way he made her feel...how just a touch from him could send her into a new stratosphere. His kisses were hungrier and made her needy and hot. Twice when he'd kissed her goodbye she wanted to beg him to stay, not to leave her hanging like this. But they were careful for now, and that was important too.

"I want you." She nodded. "I don't think I can do this much longer. This waiting part, it's causing a lot of sleepless nights and a lot of cold showers."

"We could eat later." He nodded, then shook his head. "Brayden, if you tell me no again, I might have to pull out my gun and hold it to your head to have you make love to me. I'm hurting with this."

"No guns." He stood up and began pulling off his shirt. When he dropped it on the floor as he toed off his shoes, she watched his every move. "This morning after I took my second cold shower of the day, I jerked off. It was that or go around all day with an erection. And I didn't think my mom would care for that. Besides, you know Vonda might have tried to jump me."

"Don't talk about her. Not now." He nodded and took his belt off and dropped it on his shirt and socks. "You're beautiful. I'm a little nervous now. What if I don't live up to your expectations?"

"I have very few where you're concerned. What I mean is, to me, you're perfect in every way. And I just want you to love me and be happy." Tears filled her eyes. For some reason, she thought she wasn't prone to tears, but with this man, she could let her guard down. "I'm going to pick you up and take you to bed. It won't be as big as ours will be, but I think it'll be better than the floor. Which is where I'd like to take you every time I see or touch you."

She helped him undress her. It wasn't hard. All she'd been wearing for the last few days was a large robe over a T-shirt that she was pretty sure was his. And when he dropped the robe to the floor, she felt her nipples tighten under the cotton when his eyes seemed to devour her. Instead of covering herself like she wanted to do, she lifted her chin and pushed her chest toward him.

"I'm going to enjoy making love to you." She thought she might enjoy it as well, but felt her throat close off when he took his pants off, along with his underwear. "I don't want to hurt you. I know I will, but I'll try to be easy."

"Don't be worried. Please. I need you. Inside of me. Touching me. Everything you can think of, I need it." He laughed a little and she smiled. "I want to touch you."

She didn't wait for him to reply, but wrapped her hand around his cock. He was so thick and hot that she felt her mouth water in anticipation. The thought of tasting this man, having him taste her, was almost more than she could comprehend.

"If you keep touching me like this, I'm never going to make

it so you have your pleasure first." She told him she didn't care. "Ah, but I do. Lie back, love. I want to touch every inch of you, then taste your warm flesh. Then, my cat wants his fill. Will you be all right with that?"

Would she? Dane had no idea. She did know that if he didn't touch her soon, give her what her body was demanding, she'd implode. But the moment he put his hand on her thigh, she felt her body relax, ready itself for whatever he wanted to do to her.

He dug his fingers into her muscles. It wasn't painful, but instead made her feel better. His mouth followed his fingers as he made his way down her leg to her knee. When he nipped at the back of her leg, just hard enough to send her into a whole new level of pleasure, she cried out for him to take her.

"Not yet. I have so much more of you to explore." And he did. She was thinking that later, if asked, he would be able to draw her from memory, he was getting that acquainted with her body. "You have the most gorgeous skin and freckles. I've never known a person to have freckles on their knees before. The muscles in your calves are strong and supple too. I could touch you all day and not get enough of you."

He kissed her ankles, toes, and knee. As soon as he finished with one leg, he began on the other, draining her with his touch. Exhausting her with need. The more he touched and explored her, the more she desired him, and she was sure that he knew that. And for some reason, rushing him seemed to make him take his time, touch her skin again and again until she was hurting with need.

Dane was limp with his administrations, hard with the need for completion. With each new place he discovered on her body he would take a little more of her, and she knew she wasn't going to make it. Begging him again, pleading with him to finish her, she moaned when he looked up at her from her belly, his smile not unfriendly but definitely something to be wary of, and he told her to lie still.

Before she could guess what he was doing, Brayden was gone and his cat was there. His paws were as big as her head, his teeth sharp and lethal looking. And when he moved between her thighs, Dane screamed when he licked her from gate to clit then bit down on her. The climax tore her apart and put her back together in a single heartbeat. But it wasn't enough, not nearly so, and she was hanging on for dear life when he took her under again.

With every swipe of his tongue she came screaming his name. Every time he touched his teeth to her flesh, she felt her body tumble over a cavern so deep that she was sure she would die before hitting bottom. Each climax took her higher, and every time she came she needed more. Covered in sweat and pleading again, she held onto his fur and gave him a hard yank up.

"Take me." The cat snarled at her. "Brayden, take me now or so help me, I'm going to die right here, and then where will you be?"

The man consumed the cat. Even as he was shifting, his body becoming whole, he took her mouth. He kissed her hard, his hands moving her on the bed. And when he took her, his cock filling her to the rim, she cried out again, then the world simply blinked out.

When she woke, which couldn't have been more than a few seconds later, Brayden was telling her how sorry he was. That he'd never do it again, and that he was a bastard. Dane smiled. If he only knew how he'd made her feel, she'd probably never get out of this bed. Putting her hands on his chest to make him look at her, she could see how upset he was.

"I'm so terribly sorry." She asked him for what. "I thought that I'd killed you. I swear when you fainted, all I could think about was that I'd broken you."

"You didn't, unless you count breaking me in. Then yes, you did do that." He laid his head on her chest and told her again how sorry he was. "Please stop saying that. It was wonderful. And I fainted because you were that good."

He was grinning when he lifted his head. She kissed him on the nose and felt his cock stretch inside of her. But instead of letting him move off her, she wrapped her legs around his and lifted her hips. The look on his face was complete and total pleasure.

"I'm glad that I didn't break you. I'd never be able to do this if I had." He rolled his hips again and she closed her eyes at the feeling it invoked inside of her. "Or this. This is my favorite part of making love to you. I can taste you."

His tongue ran over her chin to her throat. Dane felt her heart rate pick up and her blood run warmer through her veins. Brayden was wonderful at this, making her feel like she meant something to him. How he made her feel loved and pretty. Again, she was sure these sorts of sentiments weren't something that she had often, but that was exactly how she felt with him.

They made love slowly. He gave her all of him and more, she thought. His heart was hers, his body for sure, and she loved him as well. Something, to her mind, that she should never have expected to happen. To love and to be loved back. It was, to some degree, her thought that she'd have his love for the rest of her days, no matter what happened from here on out.

They slept for a little while after that. He held her closely, and she was sure it had to do more with what they'd just done rather than the size of the bed. And when she woke, the smells of food bringing her out of the light sleep, she found a large robe at the bottom of the bed and a single red rose. Taking the rose after dressing, she went to the office and found him putting food on the big desk.

"Sorry, I was starving after that." He grinned like a little boy. "Anytime you want to keep me from eating food by having sex, you go right ahead. I can't think of a better diet plan than to eat you instead. But come on over. Let's eat while it's hot again."

They both were starved apparently, and dug into the food like they'd not eaten in days rather than a few hours. The dumplings were wonderful, and the broccoli chicken had to be her favorite of all the things he'd picked up. There were also almond cookies, as well as tea cakes for dessert. As they drank the green tea, sipping it as their food settled, she looked at the rose again.

"I'm assuming that you didn't go out and buy that while I was sleeping." He said it was the only flower left in his mom's garden. "Yes, I was going to tell you that Vonda had been out there last night, but you distracted me."

"I thought my mom was going to be devastated when she saw what Vonda did to her garden. But she seems to be... while upset, she is going to move on from it and redo it all. I was only going to get a daisy or two for you, and that was all that's left. That woman has destroyed more in the last few days than all of us boys did together when we were children. Okay, maybe not, but she has been doing her utmost best to catch up to us. I'm thinking I'll sic my mom on her. She'll regret it soon enough, you can be sure of that." She asked if his mom was the violent type. "No. Usually she's the tap her foot and glare sort of person. It works on us. Dad too, to an extent. He just buys her flowers. I think this will take a gardener to get it back. I hate that I caused all of this."

"I don't think you did anything. Yes, you brought that woman here, but you had no way of knowing the rest. And you're working with someone to get her taken care of. So you know, if that doesn't work, then I'll gladly deal with the little shit. She's on my list too."

They sat there for several more minutes before he sat up and took her hand in his. This was serious, she could tell, and felt her breath catch at what he might be telling her. When he kissed the back of her hand, like he did when he had something important to say, Dane braced herself.

"I know what you are. For the most part anyway. I mean, not what you do but actually what you are. You're an elite shifter, as well as something more. That part I don't understand, but you're a shifter." She asked what he thought the more was. "I'm not sure. I know about shifters…I went to college with a couple of them, but you have been or you are enhanced somehow. Like you're a super shifter."

A memory slid over her mind. She'd been a mouse, trying to enter a building. She'd had to crawl along the duct work to get to someone…the same person she had thought of before. Someone important to her. She told Brayden about it.

"There is this person or something in Nelson. I have no idea why, but I need to go back and get it out. Or this person." He asked her if she wanted to wait or go now. "I'm not sure I have enough memories to get in and out right now, but I do know that it's important."

"Speaking of memories. There is this man…Christian thinks he's elderly, but he put an ad in the paper looking for you. He also filed a missing person report, but the police aren't looking into it very hard. Christian talked to him about it under the guise of asking about something else, and this man, Davie James, cried because he was so worried about you. Apparently, you play chess with him when you're not working, and you get hurt a lot."

"He and I would spend time together nightly when I was home. He did the cooking and I'd bring over the wine. I can remember him, but not what he looks like. Do you have a picture of him to help me?" He opened the computer and she went to sit with him. Before he had the computer turned on, however, he picked her up and put her on his lap. Leaning back on his chest, she watched images of every Davie James on the Internet pop up. When she recognized one, she told him to stop. "Yes, that's him. My neighbor. But.... It was a ruse, me living there. I don't remember why, but I didn't actually live in the apartment."

Dane closed her eyes, letting the face that was there fill her mind. He was there, in a vague sort of way, sitting in an old recliner. Laughing when he'd outplayed her in chess. There was a memory of him sobbing too. His son was missing.

"I know who it is. The person in the lab. It's his son, David James. I was going there to get him." As she sat there, everything about her life washed over her. What she was. What she did. And worse yet, who she was. "I'm not a nice person."

"Why?" She told him she remembered everything now. "Well, that's wonderful. Now you can get things done and straightened out for us."

"No. You don't understand. I'm not the type of person that men like you marry." He told her that wasn't fair. "Perhaps not. But I'm a hitman, in a way. I mean, Nelson literally used me to kill off people. Kidnap them to be a part of their projects. I didn't actually work for him, but for...I can't tell you that yet. It's something that I'd have to clear with this other man. But Nelson, I was working for them to get information."

"All right, but when you get permission, I'd very much

like to know who it is. But what sort of projects? As far as we can find, they only distribute drugs to pharmacies. I think they might manufacture some as well. What do they need people to die for? Or you to kidnap them?" She wasn't sure how to tell him. She had, in fact, kidnapped David and taken him to the lab for tests. "Dane, what is it?"

"They hired me to kill competitors. Or other project managers that were close to finding drugs that do what theirs does. I would only go so far in the job. I would kill, but not every time. Just when there was no other choice in the matter. But like me, for instance. I've been enhanced, as you said, but to the point where I can do this without getting caught." She put out her hand and it morphed into a long blade, the sharpness of it bright in the room. As they watched, she changed it to silver, wood, and iron. "I can kill any creature created or born with just this ability."

"Why? Why would they need you to kill anything when they're supposed to be a drug company?" She hurt with what she'd just remembered. And when he asked her again, she told him.

"I was to kill every shifter and paranormal creature there is. That way their creations, beings that they were making, could take over the world and make it their own." Brayden leaned back in the chair and said nothing. "They had this idea that once they had the shifters and paranormals all gone, that it would be a simple matter of letting their creations loose on humans that had somehow mistreated or wronged them in some way. They could and did control them with a drug they had to take daily to survive. By creating them, they had a way to easily destroy the ones that weren't living up to what they needed of them."

"And you? Do you need this drug?" She shook her head. "You're the first. They made you first and you didn't have the...."

Well, they didn't think to put a failsafe in for you. Right?"

"Yes. And they want me back to destroy me because that's the only way that they can be assured that I won't try and expose them or go there and kill them all." He didn't say anything. But then, she wasn't sure what he could have said. "I'll go as soon as I can."

"No, you won't. I don't care what they want you for or what you might have done. You aren't the same person as you were before, are you?" She said that she didn't know. "I do. And even if I wasn't so sure, you love me as much as I do you. That alone makes me know that you're not a terrible person."

She hoped he was right. But then of course, he didn't know everything yet.

Chapter 7

Vonda was getting sick of this family, and the fact that Brady wasn't doing what she wanted. How was she supposed to gain all his riches if he didn't marry her? He'd not even wanted to go shopping for a ring like she had asked about. Several times a day, in fact. She looked up when someone came into the room with her. Dr. Stanton was her least favorite person in this household.

"I see you've been making yourself a nuisance. What did you think you'd accomplish by tearing up my wife's garden like that?" She told him she had no idea what he was talking about. "Yes, you do. We know you did it because you tracked mud into the house all the way to your room. And you have cuts on your hands from tearing out the roses. Why? Why would you do that?"

"She wanted me to use her homegrown flowers in my wedding. Don't you think that is a little tacky, considering how much money Brady has? Besides, she'll get over it. It's not like she's not gaining a daughter in all this. And when we have children—and no matter what Brady says on the matter, I will have them—but when we have a child you'll forget about it too. Babies make everything all right." She thought about them ever seeing their children and knew that wasn't going to happen. "Have you seen Brady today? I thought we were going to find us a house. We can't just keep staying here with you people. I don't know if you're aware of this or not, but he can't come to my room with all of you keeping him from me. Don't you want a grandchild?"

"I think he's looking for a house, but not for you. He told me that he has a certain idea in his head about it and that's what he's looking for." He sat down when she asked him why not. "Because Brayden has no desire to marry you. I think he made that perfectly clear when he told you yesterday that he's not going to marry you. You don't listen very well, do you, young lady? He is not going to marry you, and I think you should just stop bothering him about it. In fact, why don't you go back where you came from and leave him alone?"

There was no way he wasn't going to marry her. She had plans. Vonda was going to have a new wardrobe made. There were trips she was going to take with him. The baby too. She needed a child so that he'd have to pay her monthly to keep it. Him not wanting to marry her was putting a large dent in the way things were going to go.

"He was just upset. I'll talk to him. He and I have a history of this sort of thing. Off and on like this. He'll marry me. He promised." Dr. Stanton told her that he didn't think so. Vonda knew better, so she changed the subject to something more to her liking. "I was wondering something. Why is it you've never told me to call you Dad or Mrs. Stanton, Mom? I've tried it on her and she said I was not to call her that. What about you?"

"I'd rather you didn't call me Dad. I'm not your father. Thankfully. Where is he, by the way? Your father, I mean?" She smiled. Her dad was gone, so was her mother. They had gotten in the way of what she wanted and she'd made them disappear. Permanently. "No answer, huh? Not that it matters, but you're going to have to find yourself someplace else to live that's not here. I hate being rude, but you're upsetting our household and I don't care for you. Besides, we have things to get ready for."

"I'm not leaving here until I get a ring on my finger and a nice, lovely home. As for your plans, what are they? As a part of this family, I'd think I'd be involved in them as well. I mean, we're not married *yet,* but we'll get there soon. It's a promise he made to me." Dr. Stanton only shook his head. "You never said where Brady is."

"No, I didn't, did I? I would imagine that he's doing what he wants. He has a few projects going right now, two of them are business related." She asked him why he was working. "Because he enjoys it. He's very good at it too. Brayden has been working on things since he was in middle school."

"Well, that'll have to stop as well, I think. I need him around so that we can do things together or for me. Tell me where his place of business is and I'll go and talk to him now." He told her she could rot in hell. "My goodness. Who shit in your oatmeal? Or is this about those stupid flowers? Get over it. They were a problem for me, and I'd think with all your money, you could just put in some more. It's not like they're all that special or anything. They're just flowers. That's all. Just flowers."

"They were important to my wife." She rolled her eyes at him.

Just as she was going to blast him again about being rude to her, Brady walked in the door. He looked…she thought he looked happy. And that made her happy as well. A happy Brady was a very generous Brady.

"Where have you been, darling? I've been thinking about you a lot over the last few hours. When are we going into town to shop for a ring for me?" He told her never. "You're still not upset about the stupid flowers, are you? For Christ's sake, I was just telling your father. They were only flowers. Not that big of a deal."

"We need to talk, Vonda. Now. I want to get this over with so we can move on with our lives." She smiled up at him, forever thankful that she'd seen him first that day at the party for the housing development. "If you'll come to the dining room, we'll be able to talk about a few things."

"All right. I'm glad you're finally seeing reason, Brady. I was beginning to think we were never going to have any private time. However will we have any children if you're forever running around for your family?" She was right behind him when he entered the big dining room, a place she'd been avoiding since coming here. They were just too loud for her to think when they were —

The table was set for dinner and they were all sitting around it as if they were about to have a wonderful meal. The only thing missing was the food. "What's this? I thought we were going to talk? Everyone isn't going to be here when we make our plans, Brady. I just won't have it. They'll want to do things their way. And this is my big day, not theirs."

"Have a seat, Vonda. And, like I have said to you countless times, my name is Brayden. Not Brady or any other shortened version of my name you come up with. Brayden Stanton. Say it with me." She asked him why he was being so rude. "I'm not. You are, and I've had enough of it. Have a seat."

"I won't have you talking to me this way, Brady." She said his name hard; she didn't want him to forget who was in charge right now. "Now, we're going to talk sometime when I feel like it and not today. I hope that you're happy with yourself. You've upset me. I'm going back to my room. Oh, and you had better not be buying me a little house. I know you have the money to buy me a —"

"Sit down." She found herself on a chair before she could

100

think to defy him. But he wasn't finished when he told her to shut her mouth too. "Now, I'm going to talk and you're going to listen to me. And for the love of it all, do not tell me again that I'm going to break promises to you. Had I known what sort of person you were before coming here, I would have left your ass there. I am not now, or ever, going to marry you."

"I see. You're showing off to your family. Trying to make them think you're the big man. Well, you are going to marry me, and so you know, these people will not be a part of our lives or those of our children once I get you out of here. They're a terrible influence on you. What do you have to say about that?" Crossing her arms over her breasts, she glared at him. "I don't know where you get off talking to me this way, but I'll have you know that you're not going to do it again. As of right now, things will go differently. And there is nothing you can do to change it."

"All right, if you say so. But there are things you should know. I'm not human, for one." She looked around the table and laughed. "I'm not. None of my family are. The fact that no one has killed you yet is because I've asked them not to. You have hurt my family more than enough to warrant them hurting you back."

"You're human." He shook his head. "You are. What are you trying to pull, Brady? You're not going to get out of marrying me. You made a promise. You made a promise. You made a promise. See? I can say it as many times as I want. You are going to marry me. We are going to have children, and you will buy me a big diamond because I told you to."

"I'm breaking it. There will be no diamond. No wedding, and no children. And stop calling me Brady. It's Brayden. And I'm not pulling anything. I'm not a human." She picked up the steak knife near the plate by her and stabbed it through his

101

hand and into the table. "Christ."

"See, human." The blood pooling under his hand was fascinating to her. She heard the others push back their chairs, but she didn't care. There was money on the line here, and she wasn't going to be walking away from it. "Have nothing to say, Brady?"

Brady pulled the knife out of his hand and grabbed her hand. When he put his over hers this time, she was sure he was going to stab her too. It had only been to prove a point, and now he was going to hurt her. But instead of doing that, he told her to have a look.

The hand over hers was large. She hated the way his hands were rough, but that— While she watched his hand morphed. Fur covered it. Then long nails grew from the tips of his fingers. As she continued to stare at him, his hand turned into a large paw. Like...like a giant cat. She looked at his face.

"See? Not human."

Jerking her hand from under his, she winced when his long claws tore at her skin. She was terrified, her body hot with it. And when he jerked her hand back to him, toward his mouth, she knew he was going to eat her. Instead, he licked the wounds and let her go.

Vonda staggered back from the table. Her feet tangled in the carpet and she nearly fell. Brady stood up, and she was sure that the rest of his body was going to change too. That he was going to eat her. Fear ran over her body in hot waves.

"Why are you doing this, Brady? Whatever you're doing right now, I don't find this to be the least bit funny. Is it mirrors? Some sort of drug you used on me? I don't care. We're getting married and you'll not pull this crap on me again." He told her he was a cougar. "No. That's not possible. You're a person. Like me. You're playing tricks on me."

"Are we? Perhaps you should have a look around, Vonda. There are more of us than you." She looked at the other people, and they were no longer people but big fucking cats too. She looked back at Brady when he laughed. "We're. Not. Human."

"I'm going to sue you." Brady asked her for what. "You hurt me. You cut me with your hand."

"Did I? I don't see anything." She looked at her trembling hand and saw that the cuts were gone. There wasn't even any blood on her. "Would you like for me to do that again, this time so you can watch it? The thought of hurting you as you have my mother has my cat very hungry to come out and play with you."

"Is your stupid family all you can talk about? They're nothing. They aren't like you and me. They're pitiful and not worth your time or energy. Brady, I want you to stop this right now. You'll see. Once we're married and not around them anymore, you'll see just what they are. Please, let's just go, you and I." He grinned and she could see the teeth in his mouth had changed too. They were longer, sharper than before. When fur moved over his skin, like he was going to change into this monster he said he was, she whimpered. "You're playing a trick on me. Tell me you are and we'll all laugh at it."

"No, no tricks, and I'm not going to marry you." She nodded. "No, I'm not. As I have told you for days now, I'm not going to marry you. I'm never having children with you, and even if it were possible for me to even get you impregnated, there is no way that I'd let you into my life. We're done."

Three men came into the dining room with them. She was sure they were there to tell her about the big joke that they'd played on her, but they started talking about her parents and Millner and how she was going back with them. It wasn't fair. Nothing was going her way. Picking up the knife again, she swung it around, hoping to catch someone in the act and kill them. That would make them see reason and that she was serious about what she wanted.

~~~

Brayden sat on the deck, his heart breaking for what had just happened. He wasn't allowed to change his clothing, but had to wait until they had the evidence that the police needed. She was dead...he thought that should have ended all the fact taking that they were doing, but apparently not. Christian sat in the empty chair beside him.

"A lot of people are going to get closure with this. Even those that they haven't found yet will be able to put to rest where their loved ones are." Brayden said nothing but looked at his brother. "I know you're thinking that you could have done something more. I don't know what it might have been, but you did just what the police told you and got her upset enough to make a mistake."

"She tried to kill me." Christian said that she'd not succeeded. "Yes, but she tried. She was going to cut my throat and end my life. Just because she thought I was joking with her about not getting married."

"She was insane. We all knew that." Brayden nodded. "Stop thinking about what happened out there when she tried to run. There are so many other things that you can think about and plan now. And, you can bring Dane out of hiding. At least out of the clinic downstairs. That should make you happy, right?"

"Yes. I need to talk to her, but I thought I'd wait until the police left." Christian told him to go now, he'd cover for him. "I think I will. And thank you. I don't know what I would have done if you all hadn't been there with me. She tried to kill me."

"But she didn't succeed. And now she's out of your life, permanently." She was at that. "Go. Talk to Dane and tell her what happened. She'll be there for you."

Brayden made his way to the clinic and thought about how things had gone down. It was a memory that he'd not soon forget. Nor the things leading up to it.

Patrick had come to him late last night and had shown him what they'd found in the towns that she'd been in. Also, to tell him that they were taking her back to stand trial for the murders of nineteen people and counting. Patrick told him that the death toll was growing simply because she had left them information in the things that she kept from each person in a safety deposit box in the local bank, as well fingerprints on weapons and things at her apartment that she'd taken from each home she'd been in. And they'd found a written confession of sorts from Millner, telling anyone that found him dead it would have been Vonda's doing.

"It's all there. Gloves that she and Millner used. Weapons, as well as something we're labeling as keepsakes from each of the victims. She even went so far as to label each item, as if she would someday pull it out and dream over it." Patrick had shivered and told him what the plan was. "You can piss her off, we're assuming. We've heard that once she's really pissed off, she is volatile. Like murderously so."

"You want her to kill me?" He said it would never get that far. They'd be close when she tried. "I don't know. My family will be in the house. What if you're too late and she kills me and then goes on a rampage?"

"We'll be in the house as well. And I promise you, she'll never get that close. Just upset her, make her angry, and that will be enough that we can bring her in. From there, we'll have her. All we need to connect the dots to the murders is her DNA. Then she'll go to prison whether she confesses or not. We have enough now to convict her, but a simple test will make it solid against her."

But it didn't go that way. Yes, she had tried to kill him, and when she leapt at his dad, missing him, the police had tried to take her. But somehow, and he wasn't sure how it had happened, she'd slipped by them and into the yard, where she tried to steal one of the police cruisers.

No matter how many times the police had told her to stop and to drop the weapon, Vonda kept screaming that he was going to marry her. And when she turned and threw the knife toward one of the officers, he returned fire. One shot to the head and it was over. The cop standing beside Brayden more than likely thought it had been meant for him, but Brayden knew better. The knife that she'd meant for him or his dad had stuck in the railing around the front porch, not an inch from where his dad had been standing.

When Brayden entered the clinic, his cat snarled at him. There was something wrong, they both knew it. And as soon as he saw the envelope on the bed where Dane had been, he knew that she'd left him. Sitting down, he held it without opening it. He was broken, he thought. His love had left him. But when the door to the bathroom opened he looked at Dane, who was dressed in bloody clothing that was torn and cut. Her things, he surmised.

"I didn't think you'd be back this soon." He nodded and told her it was over. "I was going to get out of here before you came back."

"I see that. And why do you think that I'd be okay with that?" She sat down and took the envelope from him and opened it. "I don't care what that says, Dane. You're my mate and I'm in love with you."

"You don't know what I do, who I am." He told her it didn't matter to him. "It should. I'm a killer. I told you that. I've

106

been trained to kill whatever I'm told. I'm a murderer, and you should never have come into my life."

"It's a bit too late for that now, don't you think?" She stood up and began to pace as he watched her. "Dane, where were you going to go? Back to the lab? I don't want you to do that. They more than likely think that you're dead. We can move on with our lives now. The police, they killed Vonda. She's...I know you know what sort of person she is...was...but she tried to kill me. Please, don't leave me."

"I'm sorry that it had to end that way, but I can't stay here. What if they find me? And no, they don't think I'm dead, but I believe they've assumed I've gone into hiding. But I'm reasonably sure that they know I'm alive." He asked her how. "When I'm out on a job, I have to bring back a part of my victim so that they can test it to be sure. Appendages are easy to remove with a switchblade and they can fit in a pocket when going through the airport. It's what they use to make sure that it's the dead guy, using DNA. As you can see, I have all my fingers and toes, so they know that no one killed me. And my tracker is gone. I'm assuming your father removed it."

"He did. It's in that machine over there." She went to the autoclave but didn't open it. "What does that have to do with this? I mean, they don't know where you are because that is gone."

"Yes. Whoever was sent to kill me would have taken that as well and turned it in when he did his job." Brayden didn't care for where this was going. "They'll come for me. And when they do, they won't stop until I'm gone."

"Please, don't leave me, Dane. Please. I've just found you and I can't live without you." She came back and sat down at the desk where he was. "I don't know what I can do to help you, but I will. Anything."

Brayden picked her up and put her on his lap. He needed to touch her, to feel her warmth against his. He knew that he was too stressed right now, and if she did leave, he'd do everything in his power to find her and bring her back. Or he'd stay with her. Whatever it took to be with her.

"I need to get into that lab, save a man if he's still alive, and then blow the place up. Preferably with people in it." He didn't say anything, but he was shocked. "If they're dead, then they can't do this to anyone else and I'll be safe. I know that sounds cold, but I want you to understand this is not a game. People are going to be killed, and I'll be responsible for their deaths. It's as simple as that, Brayden. If they're gone, then I can move on with my life. One with you if you're still willing to be with me after this."

"Yes, I am. No matter what. Vonda is dead." She asked if he'd done it. "No, the police did. They asked me to upset her enough that she would attack, then they could take her in and run some tests. But she wasn't going to stop, and they shot her when she tried to get away from them. I don't think she would have done well in prison anyway. Someone would have killed her because she didn't listen well. Dane, she was trying to kill me and my dad. I mean, she was set on it."

"I'm sorry that you guys had to go through that with her. But as you said, she's out of your life. Now I need to make sure that these people are out of mine. Do you understand that?" He nodded. "You can't help me, Brayden. You have to know that. I'm not going to allow you to anyway. You could get killed."

"Yes, I could. But if you don't let me help, then I'll go in on my own. More than likely messing up your plans as well as losing my life. Also, and I'm sure I'm correct with this, if I tell my family what you're up to, they'll want to help too. Even if they follow men in without you. So, we'll all end up dead over this. I'm thinking that you'd better let us help or no one lives."

She stared at him, then laughed. "Do you always get your way? I mean, with this line of talk? Do people just take your bullshit as gospel and give in to you?" He said not normally. "Well, I should hope not. Blackmail is not a nice way to start a life with someone."

"So, you're going to allow me to help you." She nodded and said she had no choice. "Yes, there might have been. You could have left me here without any information and I'd have been lost. Even with the note, whatever it says, I'd not know that you were going there unless you told me."

"This is a dangerously bad idea, you know that, don't you?" He did and told her so. "Then why are you willing to do this? There is no reason whatsoever that you should be involved at all."

"Yes, there is. I'm in love with you." She nodded but didn't look convinced. "Dane, when this is done, will you marry me?"

"You're so sure that it'll end with me being alive? Or you?" Brayden nodded. "You have to trust me. Do what I tell you."

"So long as you allow me to help, I'll do whatever it is you need." She said it was going to be dangerous. "Yes, I have no doubt that it will be. But as you said, we can't move on with us looking over our shoulder all the time. And on that note, I'd like for you to come and have dinner with us all tonight. My mom is cooking one of her favorite meals. Pot roast."

"You do make it hard for me to say no." He told her that was the plan. "I feel like I'm a part of your family now. They've all been down here to see me, did you know that?"

"No, I had no idea. And here I thought I was keeping the best secret ever. How did they find out you were here?" She told him. "Ah. I should have thought of that. They can smell you on me. Well, at least they know that you're my mate as well. This could be a lot of fun tonight. And I for one could use some fun after today."

He held her on his lap for a little while longer. He didn't want her to leave him. He'd have to make sure that she didn't by keeping an eye on her. And perhaps finding them a home. She'd like that, he thought. Someplace she could all her own.

As they sat there, making plans about nothing, he heard someone in the front office. He hoped it was his mom. She'd done some shopping for him. Dane stood up when his mom came around the corner.

"Brayden asked me to get you a few things while I was in town yesterday, and with all the stuff going on today.... Well, needless to say, I forgot about it until just now. Oh, and if nothing fits, it's all on me. I checked the tags in your clothing and for some reason, there wasn't any. Strange. Anyway, I had to guess. You're a little bitty thing, and I had no idea that they made such beautiful clothing. I might have to go shopping for myself soon." Dane thanked them both. "Nothing to it, really. I was out and you needed things of your own. I'll see the two of you in an hour. That's when we're eating. Brayden, there is a phone message for you in the kitchen. Wimpy took it for you earlier."

After his mom left, Dane turned to him. "Wimpy? This person's name is Wimpy?" He laughed and said that it wasn't, but that's what he'd called her as a toddler. "Her name is Wendy, but the best I could manage was Wimpy. So, it stuck. All us boys called her that, and soon Mom and Dad did as well. You'll love her. She's a wonderful cook as well as a good friend." Dane took the bag to the bathroom without letting him see what was in it. "I'll be right here when you're done dressing."

"I'm not going to leave." He heard her whistle after she closed the door, nearly in his face. "Your mom has great taste in clothing. Wow, you might not know me when I come out. Oh, and she got me a hairbrush and other things too. I love your parents."

As did he. And he hoped that he wasn't making one of the biggest mistakes of his life by offering to help Dane. He wasn't the fighter type. Brayden thought of himself more of the lay back and let things fall sort of guy. But he had a feeling that Dane had this down perfectly. Whatever she was planning.

CHAPTER 8

Christian was looking over the agreement that Brayden had given him for a new product he was upgrading. It wasn't a toy, but a way to let people with disabilities have the freedom to use computers to control their house. Such as locking and unlocking the doors. Turning on the oven to preheat or to turn it off, and to watch television. Brayden called them toys because he said that if he considered what he did work, it would take all the fun out of inventing them.

"You can't sign this. I think you knew that when you brought it to me." Brayden nodded. "Did you see the part where they will have full control over any other inventions you make that have anything to do with the handicapped?"

"Yes. But the wording was strange, don't you think? That's why I wanted you to read it. I mean, it says that I can't use the particular mechanism that makes the motors run." Christian asked him if he used that part in anything else. "Of course, it's the basis of just about any computer run program."

Christian put the contract aside and looked at his brother. "Okay, that's out of the way. What really brought you in here? Because I know you spotted that right off or you'd have signed it regardless of what I had to say. What's up?"

"She's going back to that lab." Christian had already figured that out. When he was told that Dane had all her memories back, he knew that she was going to finish whatever had gotten her into trouble in the first place. "I told her that we would help her. No matter if she left me behind or not."

"Good." Brayden looked shocked for a few seconds, then laughed. "You really didn't think we'd just let her go, did you? I mean, you're in the best mood, other than today, that I've ever seen you in. And you're home for good, which I think has Mom and Dad thrilled beyond words. And I like her. I mean, I really like her. She's smart, despite wanting to be with you. I like the way her mind works. Not in a straight line, but in more of an out of the box sort of way."

"I know. She isn't a talker either, which I enjoy. No emptying of her mind to hear her voice. When she says it's figured out, then you can bet that it is. But I can't get my head wrapped around this thing with her. I mean, I can understand that she wants to take care that we're not always looking over our shoulder for someone coming for her. But they haven't yet. She's been at the house for about a month now, and nothing."

Just as Christian was about to comment, his phone rang and when it came up blocked, he nearly didn't answer it. But he figured that he could think of a good answer to Brayden while whoever it was prattled on about the product that he needed for his office. He answered on the third ring.

"Mr. Stanton? It's Davie James. I wanted to talk to you about Dane." He motioned for Brayden to be quiet and put it on speaker phone. "You said you'd help me when we talked a while back. And I was wondering if your offer still held up. I'll pay you what you asked."

"Yes, Mr. James. I was hoping you'd get back to me. What kind of help did you need for me to do? I'm open to all suggestions." He made a noise that sounded to Christian like a small sob. And when he blew his nose too, Christian knew he was crying. The poor man. "You know that I'll have to see you in person, correct? That was the arrangement that we made. Money up front before I can help you."

"Yes. Yes, I remember now. Yes. I can meet with you...." Christian could hear someone talking; their voices were low, but with his hearing, he knew that the elderly man wasn't alone. "I can meet with you tonight. Come over to my house. I have some of Dane's things that I can sell you, too. If you want them."

"Of course I do. They might come in handy when looking for her." The man said thank you four times, as if he really was grateful that he was coming. "I'll be there around five, is that all right with you? I'll also need your address so I don't get lost."

After exchanging the information, the call was disconnected. Christian looked at Brayden and thought about the conversation that they'd been having before the call. He decided they'd all need to help her, just as he'd suggested.

"There's something wrong. With that man, I mean. I think he was trying to give me hints. Brayden, I never offered him money. Nor did I say I would help him find her. I only suggested that he get some help through the police." Brayden asked him what he'd meant by some of her things. "I have no idea. But there might be something in those things that will help us figure out why they want her so badly that they'd have an old man call me for it."

"You think that they found out somehow and are trying to get you there for information?" Christian nodded. "This isn't good. Not at all. Dane told me that they would know that she was alive and that they'd come for her. I guess she's right."

"The problem now is, what do I do? I'm supposed to go and meet this guy at his house to help him and to buy some of the things that may or may not belong to Dane. For all we know, it

115

has a tracking device in it so that they can figure out where we live so they can come here looking for her." Christian wasn't being paranoid, but he was sure he was right. "We have to get help. I'm an attorney, and while that makes me somewhat of a criminal in a few people's minds, this is way out of my league."

"Yes. Help from Dane. I don't think there is anyone more suited to do this than her. As much as I hate to get her hurt, I don't think we have a choice in the matter." Christian wasn't so sure. They'd already hurt her once, and said as much to Brayden. "Yes, they did. But this time she'll know up front what is going to happen, because we're going to have a plan. With her."

While Brayden went to find Dane, Christian finished up some paperwork, and also called the Med-Corp people to tell them that Brayden was going to pass on signing the contract with them. After being transferred around several times, having to repeat his story each time a new person answered their phone, he was connected with the president of the company.

After explaining yet again that Stanton Products wasn't interested in doing business with their company, the man laughed. Christian was ready to hang up when the man started speaking again.

"Don't want to do business with us? What sort of person decides to give up millions of dollars over the next fifteen years by not wanting to do business with a company?" Christian said a billionaire did. "Are you telling me that the man who invented this little doodad is a billionaire? I don't think so. I want you to tell your client that we don't do hardball tactics. He either signs the agreement or he's going to be out of luck. We take our jobs very seriously here, and he'll learn that soon enough."

"In the event that you misunderstood me, Stanton Products isn't going to be playing with you at all. Also, he is not going to sign any contracts with your company now or in the future. So your threats of him hard-balling you are unfounded. He has not once asked for more money, nor did he ask for any sort of compensation." Christian tried to calm his temper, but he'd had enough of this company already and let the man have it. "The next time you threaten a client you'd better have all your ducks in a row, and make sure that the conversation isn't being recorded as this one is. And just in case you have it in your head to tell me that it's not legal, you should go back to the very first person I talked to and listen to the prerecorded message that they get when a phone call, either in or out of my office, is made. It says that all conversations will be recorded."

"Now see here, you can't talk to me that way. And I want you to tell your client that he'd better not be selling to my competitors. I will not be run out of business by a snot nosed boy and his ten dollar an hour attorney." Christian laughed…it felt good too. "What the fuck do you think is so funny?"

"You are. And it's been a pleasure talking to you. I'll make sure that I mention your name to a lot of my ten dollar an hour friends as well. I'm sure that you will be the butt of a great many jokes at the table from now on. You have a nice day."

Christian hung up on the blustering man. He laid his head on the desk and closed his eyes. It was getting harder and harder to be polite to people, whether in person or on the phone, he thought. In his opinion, everyone believed that their shit didn't stink. He was just thinking about quitting his work, holing up in some cave somewhere and living off the land, when Brayden and Dane entered the office. He looked at her and smiled. It was amazing what the love of a good person could do to someone.

"You look lovely, my dear. Must be all that good rest you're getting. And I'm to understand that the two of you are looking for a house." She snorted at him and told him to behave. "I've just gotten off the phone with one of Brayden's clients. I don't think you want to see what I'm really feeling right now."

"You should get a punching bag." He looked at Brayden then back at Dane when she continued. "It's either get something you can take your frustrations out on so you can live better, or get yourself a hooker to come in and relieve it for you. Either one will have the same effect. Though, I would think that the getting laid part would do you one better."

Christian stared at her for several seconds before he burst out laughing. She had, in one statement, made all his anger slip away. He was thinking that he'd have to be on his toes around her, and almost felt sorry for his brother. Dane was not the type of woman that Brayden normally dated. But the best part was, she was going to give him a reason to laugh, and that to him was a good thing.

"I've just gotten off the phone with Davie James. You know him." She nodded, even though it wasn't a question. "He might be in trouble. There was someone there with him, and he asked me to buy some of your things that he has. I don't know what that means."

"They must have found out about him because of his son. I would say that when you called him, his phone was tapped. That's what I'd do. What did he say, exactly?"

He told her everything that had happened, as well as the voices that he'd heard in the background. Christian knew that Brayden had more than likely told her too, but she listened to him as well as asked questions. When he was finished, he asked her what Mr. James might have that belonged to her.

"The key to a safety deposit box. In it are notes, contracts, as well as photos of the lab and what they're up to. He doesn't know what's in the safe, just that it's important that it shouldn't fall into the wrong hands. By him telling you that he has things to sell of mine, he's saying that he's not told them about it, but worries. He's giving me a heads up…if you know me, you should tell me to go and get my things before it's too late. I have a key as well." Brayden asked if they should go and empty it. "Yes. But I will, you two will not be going. And before you argue, you should listen to me. They might not know about the bank and box, but if they do, then they're going to be waiting for me to show up. It won't matter if you are with me or not. If you're near enough to them when they see me, you'll be dead. As will any other person in the place. I need to go in without them knowing and get out the same way."

"And why would you be in less of a situation if we don't go?" She didn't answer him, but bent at the waist to her boots. Christian had seen them before…he'd helped his dad remove them from her. But instead of the knife that he knew was there, she pulled out a gun as well as a scary looking knife. Not at all the one he'd seen before. "That makes you well armed. But will it be enough?"

She continued to empty pockets and places on her clothing that he'd not noticed. There were more guns and knives. A stack of throwing stars made of what appeared to be silver. Magazines for the guns. A roll of wire that he didn't want to think about what she needed it for, as well as several vials of some blue liquid that he didn't want to know about either. He looked up at her when she sat down.

"You're a bad mother fucker, aren't you?" Dane grinned at him. "I'm just going to assume that you can use all these without any problem, and that any death that is incurred because of them will be justified."

"Of course it will be. I'm not completely heartless. But as I was saying, I can get in and out of the bank much quicker and more safely than all of you can. I can promise you too, that should there be trouble, or issues as you called them, there won't be after I walk out the door." Christian didn't doubt that one bit. "I can do this. I know which box I'm going to, where the key is, as well as do things you can't even imagine. Also, being a shifter will make it so no one sees me unless I want them to. I'm the safest bet when it comes to this part of the job."

"All right. Say you get in and out. Then what?" That's what Christian wanted to know, and was glad that Brayden asked her. "I mean, do you go to the house then? Are Christian and I going to go while you take care of the bank? I'd really like to know at least some of this plan of yours. Not that I don't think you can handle it, but it would go a long way in giving me added security if I had some details."

"They're only expecting Christian at the house. If anyone else shows, especially if they look as much alike as you guys do, then there will be trouble. I'm not saying you can't be close to him to help, but going there in the open will get all of you killed." Christian thought that was a good thought. "When he goes, I'll be with him. In his pocket."

Christian didn't even ask. However she was going to pull off that feat, and he had no doubt that she would, then he'd be glad for the company. But he was worried about Brayden. The man was in love with his mate, and wouldn't enjoy being left behind.

~~~

Scurrying across the floor, Dane watched the men in the doorways. There were three in the big building that didn't belong, and she was positive that they were holding some of the bank workers hostage until she showed up. Their knowing about the safety box gave her the idea that Mr. James was no longer living. They would have had to kill him to get the information from him. He'd told her once that he'd been tortured by the best when he'd been in the service, and if he didn't break with them, he wouldn't with these goons either.

As a mouse she was able to move quickly without being seen. It didn't worry her overly much that anyone would notice a little rodent, but she was concerned about how she was going to get into the safe room. The door, usually left open during the day with a guard at the entrance, might be her only stumbling block as far as she could see. She wondered what they'd done with the people who worked there, or if they were already dead.

The door, just as she had suspected, was closed. There were no men at it...another reason that she knew these men were unfamiliar with this particular branch. Watching the goings on, she realized that there was another way she could get in. She moved down the hall to the elevators and quickly changed to a human. Pulling the fire alarm, she became a mouse again and waited. The vault would remain closed after they left, but that wouldn't be a problem for long. The bank manager would have to stay behind if there was no immediate smoke or fire to put the cash drawers in the safe. It was a long shot, but one that she thought would work.

As the people started to scramble around to get out of the building, she stayed as close to the vault as she could. Then just as she was ready to think this wasn't going to work, the bank manager came to the vault and opened it to take in the drawer from the single teller. She slipped in behind him.

It took the man less than two minutes to put the drawer in and leave her to her business. She knew there were cameras in the room, so she stayed well behind them when she shifted to human once again. One of the things that she'd not shared with the others was that when she went from any being to the next, she still had her clothing. It was one of the things that the lab had wanted her for. That, and a plethora of many other abilities

121

she had.

She could also put things on her person and keep them with her. It wasn't something that she did a lot of—mostly it was weapons or such—but the key, her key that was a copy of the one that Davie had, was in her pocket. Taking it out when she had disabled the cameras, she inserted it into the large box and took out another key from the false bottom. She had less than thirty seconds to open the real box that had her things in it.

She knew this bank like her own home. There would be, at exactly one minute, a safety mechanism engaging. A long steel rod, six inches thick, would drop down the back of all the boxes and loop into the hole at the back of each drawer. Locking the drawers into their slots so that they couldn't be pulled no matter what had been a stroke of genius. Also, a pain in the ass when someone like her needed to get in and out quickly.

Dane knew what was in the box, and if it ever fell into the wrong hands, she'd be fucked and so would a great many other people. She'd put it all in here herself over the years, and in the same way she had gotten in and out today. As she emptied it, taking all the photos as well as her many passports out of it, she was reminded of her promise to Davie. He wanted his son home.

David James, Davie's son, wasn't a lab rat like she was. He was one of the lab techs, and not by choice. He'd been taken there, by her, to do a job. But her understanding was that he was going to be released when he had completed whatever project they had need of him for. But after a couple of weeks, not only was he chained to his lab equipment, but he was also put in a cage nightly to keep him from escaping.

It had worked for a while until he started to get smart. Or stupid. It depended on who you asked. But after a few months, David had stopped eating and working. They weren't so concerned about the first part, but the last one had pissed them off. He got so weak that he wasn't able to do anything but lie in a bed. That was when she went to talk to him.

"You live until I can come back for you, and I will, then I'll take you out of here. You have my word on that." He told her to go away. "I know your father."

That woke him up. He looked at her with strained eyes, beaten and overtaxed. "You're lying. You brought me here. Why should I believe anything you say to me?"

"Your dad is my friend. And if you want to believe it, I'm just as trapped as you." She told him about the drug they gave her every day, how it kept her heart beating and her body viable. "I have to do what they tell me to a point. But I'm done with them. All of this shit."

"You don't need the drug. What you take is only a placebo." She shook her head. "I make it for you. I know what's in it. You have no idea how tempting it's been for me to kill you with one of the many poisons here. But I must make two of them, and one of the guards holds a gun to my head while one of them takes the other one. When they live, so do I. I wish now that I had just done it for us both."

Every day for two weeks she went to see him, telling him that she was going to come back for him. But nothing worked until she had his dad write him a letter. After that, she had convinced him that he needed to live, if for no other reason than to go back to his father. During that time, however, she stockpiled the pills she was given and never had anything change about her health or her body. It wasn't the first time that they'd lied to her, but it was the last time that she would believe a single word that spilled from their mouths. And there had been plenty of bullshit.

When she had loaded all her things in the many pockets on

her clothing, she moved to the small vent hole that was letting in the fresh air. It scared her a little, to crawl into such a small space, but she knew that this was going to be the least of her worries once she got out. After ten minutes of running as fast as she could, Dane was standing outside the bank. Brayden was right there waiting for her when she shifted.

"You didn't set the place on fire, did you?" She assured him that she hadn't. "Good. I'd hate to have to figure out where to go for a loan for our house when the only bank in town is closed."

He was joking, of course, but she would have to tell him soon that there wasn't any reason for them to get a loan if they didn't want to. She had more than enough money. But then, she supposed he did as well. The man was as wealthy as she was, it appeared.

As they made their way to the lab, Dane gave him all the things she'd gotten. "Make sure that you keep them away from the lab. And that would mean away from anyone that you might know too. Anyone could be a part of this thing for enough money." He told her that he would keep it safe. "I'm going to get out of this, with David, but things will be bad for a little while. What I'm going to do, it's not going to be pretty. But you have to keep Davie safe, if you can."

"You think he's dead." She told him about the guards in the bank, and that the deposit safes she'd opened would be noticed soon. "All right, but you be safe too. I don't want anything to happen to you either."

The change in plans bothered her some. She wasn't going to be with Christian when he went to Davie's house, but going to the lab instead. Time, she knew, was running out for a lot of people. Especially David and herself.

"I don't want anything to happen to any of us. But I made a

promise and I intend to keep it." He kissed her when they were only a few miles from the lab. When she got out, she turned and kissed him again. "When this is done, you will need to know everything that I am. Some of it is good, others not so much."

"I don't care so long as you're in my life." She nodded and looked at the sky, then back at Brayden. "You're a shifter, I get that. Do what you need to do to get this done."

Shifting to an eagle, she took to the skies. It would be over soon, but she wasn't so sure that Brayden would be able to handle it. Dane was going to kill the people in the lab and then destroy it. It was the only way to be sure that nothing else like her would come out of the place.

CHAPTER 9

Peter Nelson listened to the salesman drone on about how they were going to be able to make millions with a drug he was proposing they produce. Peter no longer cared if they made a drug that was going to save the world from itself. He had bigger and better plans for his building.

"So, as you can see, there is a real way we can beat this disease if we can work together on this. I've been trying my best to get this run through the market, but no one sees the whole picture." Peter picked up the proposal and read the top line. It was a drug to take care of ingrown toenails? "There are a lot of people that have to suffer in silence with this. All it would take is a person with the visionary foresight that someone like you has to make it go away."

"I see." He really didn't, but wanted the man gone. He had more important things to do than just sit around talking about the state of someone's feet. "I'll have my lab team look this over. And then in a few days, no more than a couple of weeks, I'll have someone call you to see if we can work something out."

When hell froze over, he thought to himself. There was no fucking way he was going to use his valuable time in trying to figure out how to make someone's toes better. After seeing the man to the front desk, he made his way back to the lab. There was shit going on today that needed his attention. He entered just as the man that had been strapped to the chair last night was being hit again.

"Well, this looks like it's going well." The man that he'd created six years ago looked at him. It was scary, seeing his face without the mask he was required to wear. But he smiled, and that made it even more chilling.

His face was a mass of muscles that had grown at different stages of the process. The left cheek was grossly out of proportion to the right. His eye was an inch or so higher on the left because of it. Bogo, what they had all started calling him when he'd been born, wasn't able to speak, and as far as Peter knew, he had to be dressed and bathed like he was an infant as well.

But he was strong, and because of something that had occurred in the process, he was also single minded. Once you told him something to do, but only one thing at a time, he would do it until he dropped. Like today, he had been told to hit the man before him when he heard a bell ring. And from the looks of the old man, Bogo wasn't holding back.

"Has he said anything more than just a bank deposit box? It's costing me a fortune to keep men at each bank in hopes that she shows up for her shit. Damn it, why didn't she just fucking die?"

"How do we know that she's not dead?" Peter looked over at his partner and wanted to pull a gun and shoot him as well. Damian Sams had been a pain in his backside for the last four years. "I mean, you said yourself that there has been no movement on the tracker. That she's not been seen nor heard from for weeks. For all you know, she and this guy you sent for her are both rotting in some landfill together and we won't know it. We need to get moving on shit, Peter. There is money to be had here, and I want it coming in. I've done my part, when is yours going to be over?"

"Have you seen this tracker, Damian? After we sent out Mark to kill her, did it move? I mean, last I heard there was nothing on it. Not even a blip after the first day. How do we know that she's even wearing it any longer?" Damian said nothing but did shrug, a body movement that could set Peter off faster than anything. "Don't act like this is nothing. She knows a great deal. And has a mindset that will get all of us killed should she desire it."

"Yet, as you have said yourself, we've heard nothing from her. Like I said, she's dead and we have nothing to worry about. This man here, all he's given you is that she had a safety box that he has a key for. Nothing about where the bank is or what might be in it, nor what she was going to do with it once she got it. I would have thought that had he known anything, someone would have figured it out by now." They both looked at Davie James. The man had taken a beating, that was for sure. "He's about gone. What do you hope to accomplish by killing him too?"

"She's going to pay." And she would be more pissed when she found out what they'd done to this man, too. "I don't believe for a moment that she's going to die for us. She might be hurt, but there is no way that Dane is dead. That would be just too easy for me."

Peter was terrified of Dane. Not just because she was stronger, but also because she had no compulsion about killing someone if she felt that it was justified. If it needed to be done, she'd be the first one to draw her gun, shift, or whatever it took to get the job done. And then drink a beer or two with the people that might have seen her do it. Dane Mueller was a fucking badassed killer. And what she did to some of the dead had him waking up in the middle of the night drenched in sweat. She was coming for them, he knew it.

There was a knock at the door to the interrogation room, and he bid enter to the man on the other side. It took Peter several tries to get him to speak before he looked away from Bogo. When he finally did, Peter was sure that he was going to piss himself.

"It's moving." Damian asked him what was moving. "The tracker. It moved for about a minute, then as I was coming here to get you, it stopped again. I don't know what's going on, but it moved about forty miles before it stopped again."

"Christ. Which direction?" The kid told him toward here. "Of course, she's fucking coming for us. She's on her way here, and we can't do shit about it."

"Of course we can. We just have to kill her before she gets in. I've taken it upon myself to hire a few extra guards in the event she came around. Looks like you were right all along." Peter thought that when this was done, if he lived, he was going to kill that mother fucker, Damian. "We'll have to stop this fun for now or kill him. Which do you think?"

"Save him. He might be our only bargaining tool since you killed his son." Killing David, he knew now, had been a mistake. Not only was the man's research gone with him, but he had only recently found out that Dane had been his friend. He was sure that was just going to make her day as well.

He followed the kid to the computer base. It had been Damian's idea to have a computer room like this one. A way to track the news, the police, and any of their creatures that they sent out on a job. Most of the time it was boring, he supposed. But lately, since Dane had decided to leave them, the place had been hopping.

Why she had gotten it into her head that she could survive on her own was still something that he was trying to figure out. He thought that David, or someone else, had told her that the drugs the others needed didn't work on her, but he wasn't so sure. It was him that she'd gone after that afternoon, and Peter would never forget, not so long as there were mirrors that he could see into, what she'd done to him.

The stitches had been close and tight, but he knew that he'd wear her mark for the rest of his life. Her cutting him had gone from his left ear through his cheek, slicing into his fleshy fat all the way to the teeth, then to the middle of his throat. At first, they worried that he'd never talk again, but even though his voice was gravely and he slobbered like a baby, he was able to speak. And that was a good thing. For both of them.

He looked at the computer monitor and tried to figure out what he was seeing. A map, yes. He could make that out, but there wasn't anything there. Then he saw it, the red dot that he was told was Dane. As he watched it, it moved quickly, making him think that she was flying, then it just disappeared. As he was trying to get someone to tell him where it had originated, it started up again on another computer.

"Where is she now?" No one answered him, and he had a feeling that he didn't want to know. "How close is she to here?"

"Outside the front gate, it seems." He asked him if she was moving. "No. She's just standing there as far as we can see. Do you want me to let her in?"

Peter hit the man on the back of the head. The fucking idiot. Let her in? Fuck. Didn't he get it? If she wanted in, she'd be there. And Peter had a feeling that she was already where they were, and there really wasn't a damned thing he could do about it. The boy at the computer asked him what that had been for.

"No, I do not want you to let her the fuck in. Do you have a death wish? She's fucking here to kill us all." The kids, because that's what all of them who worked here looked like, stood up. "Sit down until I tell you that you can leave. And if she moves,

I want to know about it."

He made his way to his office, keeping an eye out for anything that might be there. As far as he knew she couldn't shift into objects, but it would be just like her to not tell them when she figured it out. The fucking bitch was forever making them look stupid when she was here. Now she was free, and had more than likely figured out a great many things he'd just as soon she didn't know.

As soon as he was in his office, he locked the door. As he turned, he realized what she'd done.

"Hey there, moron. You have got to be one of the stupidest bad men I've ever encountered, you know that, don't you? The tracker that you put on my body is outside. I thought it would be a bit more fun for me to come in here without you being aware. You were though, weren't you, Peter?" He nodded and felt his balls tighten to his body when she put out her hand and it changed into a long, slim blade. "We're going to have a little talk, you and I. Then I'm going to kill you."

"Why? I made you what you are, you stupid cunt. Why would you want to kill your creator?" The pain took his breath away and he staggered to the seat when she told him again to sit. The star, a metal circle that had sharp points in it, was sticking out of his right arm. "You're fucking going to pay for that."

"And how do you suppose that is going to work? Are you perhaps hiding an army in your pocket? Or do you think that I'm going to allow you to call someone to come in here and *try* to kill me? Try is all they're going to be able to do, Peter. I've had enough of your bullshit, lies, and just plain fuckery." He pulled the star out of his arm and thought about throwing it back at her, but he stopped when she smiled. When he laid it on the desk, she pouted. "Oh, well that is no fun. Don't you want to play, Peter? I think that with my hands unchained, I can do some pretty amazing shit, don't you?"

"You were never meant to be able to think on your own." She said that she had already figured that out. "What do you want? Money? I have a great deal of it."

"No. Money means nothing to me. At least not at the moment. You see, I'd rather you put me back the way I was." He told her that was impossible. "Then I guess I'll have to settle for your death. While not as satisfying, it will be fun for me."

When she stood up, he felt his bladder let go. He was terrified of her and always had been. She was strong, smart, and lethal. He wasn't sure of what her plans were for him, but he had no doubt that he really was going to die. And whatever they were, Peter had a feeling that it wasn't going to be quick or painless. She was out for his blood.

~~~

Brayden could feel her fear. She wasn't terrified, but she was afraid. Of what, he had no idea. But he refrained from asking her so he'd not distract her from her task. He had yet to tell her that the house that Christian had gone to was empty, and that he doubted the man living there was still alive. The police said that it looked like one hell of a struggle had ensued.

I'm in. Brayden felt himself relax a little, and the breath that he'd been holding whoosh out of his lungs. *Such a worrywart. I told you that I'd be all right.*

You did, but that doesn't mean I won't worry until you're back here. Are you all right? Really? She told him she was talking to Peter now. *Talking or killing?*

Talking. But that won't last for long. I found David. He's dead. And Davie is here as well, but I don't think he's going to make it. They've worked him over pretty good. I'm not going to say that I don't understand it, but it doesn't make it any easier to comprehend. He was...both of them were good men. He told her he was sorry. *Me too. I'm going to hang out here for a bit. I want to make sure that Peter knows that he's fucked with the wrong person, and then I must find Damian. He's a sadist that needs to be shown the error of his ways.*

He didn't ask. He could have, he knew that, but she'd tell him, and Brayden was sure that he'd have nightmares for a very long time if he knew what she had in mind. Instead, he told her about the house that they were going to live in.

I hope you're okay with it. I had to do something while we were just standing around. And I think we got a good deal. She told him that she had money should he want to just pay cash. *No. Christian assures me that we need to make a few payments on it. As a tax deduction. And he's going over the paperwork for me. Again, while we wait. Oh, and Levi wants to know if he can paint you. And before you agree, he means in the nude. I'm not so sure about that.*

She laughed and he smiled. *I'd love for him to paint me. And I'll give it to you as a gift. Well, babe, I should get busy here. I'm not sure how long I'll have before someone comes looking for this jackass. I've made a few calls and there will be police arriving at some point, though I don't think they'll have anything to do with this.*

Why is that? She didn't answer, so he didn't ask again. *I love you, Dane. I needed you to know that. You're the best thing that has ever happened to me.*

And you to me. I have to go now. Peter has wet himself, and rather than finding that funny, I find it sad. He made me what I am, and now he's pissing himself in fear.

The connection was closed but he could still feel her. She was gaining her confidence back. Not that he had any trouble believing that she was as strong as she needed to be. But having confidence in oneself was more than half the battle when trying to do something you might not be sure of.

The police were still in the house when Christian said his

name. As they stood watching, his brother handed him a key. He had no idea what it was until he pointed to the apartment next to the one where the police were.

"She said to give it to you. And while I have no idea what you might find in her apartment, I want you to know that I expect you to take pictures. I have a feeling that she's as sloppy as Levi is, and has empty pizza boxes everywhere." He laughed with Christian. "She also said to tell you that there is a safe under the bed. She'll give you the combination for it when you find it. And there are weapons as well. I don't know where, but I'm assuming everywhere, knowing her."

"What's in the safe, did she tell you?" Christian said he had no idea. "All right. But if there is a body, I'm never forgiving you for this. She is scary, don't you think?"

"Yes. But she loves you, and that makes her all right in my book." Brayden hugged his brother as he made his way down the hall to the door that he'd been told was hers. Putting the key in the lock, he was almost afraid to open it. For all he knew there could be bad guys on the other side. Or a trap. But then, she would have told him. *If* she remembered it. Brayden was scaring himself and decided that wasn't good.

The door slid back on its hinges without a sound. It was creepy, really. Brayden felt like he was in a horror flick and that he was going to be murdered by some masked man. He felt her humor before she spoke to him.

You have a very strange thought process. Or you watch too many scary movies. You're a cougar...aren't you scarier than anything on the television? He told her it was her fault. *Mine? I'm not even there with you and you're afraid that someone is going to kill you. Honey, had you been a target, you'd have been dead by now.*

You know, believe it or not, that's not the least bit helpful. She laughed again and he felt his fear slide away. Then he looked

135

around the tiny place. *I think that Christian is going to be very disappointed. He expected you to be a slob.*

No, not at all. I don't spend a lot of time there, so I try not to have to come back to a mess. There are some things that I want you to get for me that are important. Also, you should find the safe. It's got money in it. A great deal. He told her he'd get that first. *I need to go. I'm having too much fun here. And no, before you ask, I've not spilled a drop of his blood. Yet.*

Before she closed their connection again, he got the combination to the safe and was told where he could find a bag. Or several as it turned out. He looked around her place and was amazed at what he found.

She wasn't a slob. In fact, she might border on being too organized. Everything wasn't just put into place, but was labeled and color coded. He opened the cabinet in the kitchen to see three boxes of the same cereal with the dates of expiration clearly written on the side of them. The fridge was empty of everything but an apple that was clearly too old to eat, and the freezer had a single ice tray in it with one cube missing. He had a feeling that she only used them one at a time so it would be neat.

The next room was the living room. There was a lonely chair, a reading lamp, as well as a stack of books, mostly classics, and a couple of them looked to be rare. As he stacked them up again, he looked for a television and wasn't surprised not to see one. She didn't strike him as a movie buff either.

An office contained nothing but a desk and chair. There wasn't a computer, again no television, and not a single picture hung on the wall. He realized that the house was devoid of any kind of art, including a calendar. He decided to ask her about that when he saw her.

The bathroom was sterile…there wasn't any other way to

describe it. A single white towel hung on a hook behind the door. A white shower curtain hung by the tub, and a bar of equally white soap was in the dish. The shampoo was the only bit of color in the entire room, and it was in a pale pink bottle that he might have missed had he not moved the shower curtain.

No toothpaste or brushes of any kind marred the counter. Everything was in the top drawer marked dental. He wondered about that as he made his way into her bedroom.

It was sad. He realized that as soon as he walked it. Again, nothing on the walls. The bed, a single, was made military style without a wrinkle in it. The sheets were white, he could see, and the wool blanket was army issue, he'd bet. It was green, a nasty color he thought, with a darker green stripe down the bottom of it. A pillow was laying on the bed, not propped up as his always was, and there wasn't a lamp or another book on the nightstand. Just an alarm clock, as well as a charger for a phone.

Lifting the mattress up to find the safe, he laughed when he saw that it was attached to the bed frame and not under the flooring as he had thought it would be. Of course, he thought, she'd be different in even this. As he used the numbers that she'd given him on the keypad, he was careful not to disturb anything else. Because along with the safe, there were three rifles of varying types, as well as numerous handguns and other paraphernalia, attached to the bottom of the frame. If anyone came into her place with ill will, they'd be dead before they crossed over the threshold.

Going back to where the bags were hanging, again in neat order, he grabbed several more. Brayden gathered all the handguns and ammunition and put them into one of the heavier bags. Then he removed all the others, including the rifles, and put them on the floor next to him. Then he took out the money from the safe.

There was a great deal of it, as she'd told him, all in hundreds; he'd bet that there was close to ten million in the thing. He wondered why she'd have cash, then realized that no one would pay her with a check because of what she was. A killer. Christ, to have had to live like that must have been hard, he supposed.

When he had it all stacked in the bags, he tried to figure out how to get the guns out of the apartment with a bunch of cops just outside the apartment. The knock at the door startled him, and he went to see who it was. Christian said it was him.

"Mom and Dad are here with the rest of our brothers. Dane said you'd need us." He nodded and let them all in. "Christ. I was so wrong. It's nice, isn't it? And boy, she is neat."

"Yeah, she said that you'd be happy to know she's not a slob. I have to get her things out of here before the cops come. Do you mind helping?" Everyone said that they'd be glad to, and he took them to the bedroom. "I don't know how to get them out of here short of throwing them over our shoulder and announcing to the world what we're carrying."

"We'll just put them under our clothing." He asked his mom how that was going to work. "Let me show you. I saw this on a movie once. I thought it quite clever."

It took them ten minutes to get all the rifles put in their pants. He had no idea what sort of things his mom was watching, but was glad that she'd seen this. He loaded the handguns and all the magazines into three more bags, because one bag was just too heavy. He and his brothers carried those out. The money and jewelry from the safe was with him as well. Christ, if they were stopped or pulled over, they were all going to prison, he just knew it.

They weren't stopped as he had worried they would be.

And when everything was loaded into his parents' car, they headed home. He had never been so glad to see them leaving him behind as he was then. They had enough weapons and ammo in their car to start and win a small skirmish.

He was just going back to where Christian had parked his car when one of the officers came to talk to them both.

"There is no sign of Mr. James. A lot of blood that we're looking into, but we have no way of knowing if it's his or belongs to a couple of people." Brayden thanked him. The officer looked at his brother. "You said that you came here for a meeting. Can you tell me what it was about?"

"His son is missing. I'm sure that you've heard about that." The officer said that it was still an open case. "I saw something about it the other night on the computer and offered my assistance. As an attorney, I have a lot of contacts, and I thought that if we worked together, we might have a happy solution for him. Do you know anything about the case that you can share? I really do want to give him as much help as I can to get his son back."

"David has been missing for a couple of months. Last I heard, Mr. James had put out a reward. If it was anyone else but you, Mr. Stanton, I'd wonder if you had anything to do with taking the man for the money. But I thank you for offering to help him." Brayden wondered what the cop meant and figured it out when he continued. "I'm sure that putting up that sort of reward would bring in a lot of people trying to make a quick buck or two off him."

One million, he found out later. The man had put out a one-million-dollar reward for the return of his son. He wondered how he could have managed that, but thought that it would have mattered little to him if he got his child back. Such love knew no bounds.

139

It was another twenty minutes before they were allowed to leave. Instead of going home, he asked Christian to take him by the lab. He had made a promise not to go in, but there wasn't any reason he couldn't have a little drive by. Brayden was worried about Dane, and he wanted to be close enough to help her, but knew that he'd be more of a hindrance than a help to her in this sort of situation. He would just have to trust her. And he did, but that didn't mean he wasn't worried too.

CHAPTER 10

Damian could hear the screams from where he was hidden. He didn't dare try to leave again. He'd only just gotten around the corner when he saw Dane moving toward Peter's office. And now here he sat, curled up under one of the desks in a lab, holding his breath every time someone walked by the door.

The inmates were loose. He had seen it on the link from his phone. They all had trackers on their person, but for whatever reason, he couldn't make the stupid failsafe go off. The tiny detonator was supposed to blow up when he pressed in a code and it wasn't working. He had a feeling that Dane had done that as well.

It had been his idea, unbeknownst to Peter, that the trackers were also a way to destroy the monsters they'd created. Peter thought them to be just a way to make sure that they were going where they were assigned and returning when they were told. Damian, and a now dead tech guy, had come up with the wire to the heart too. Once the code was pressed in correctly, the tracker would explode and a small wire that was attached to the heart muscle would set off a secondary explosion that would kill the host. But that did him little good if he couldn't get the piece of equipment to work correctly. If he got out of this, and he hoped that he would, he was going to have someone tell him what went wrong.

The knock at the door had him holding his breath again. He wasn't sure which of the monsters would knock, but he waited. When the door opened slowly, he closed his eyes. It wouldn't keep him from being found, but he didn't want to see what was coming after him or what they had in way of a weapon. He heard someone just as the door closed quietly, and opened his eyes and whimpered.

The large cougar startled him. Damian pressed his back against the desk and felt it move under his weight. The cougar came closer and was looking him directly in the eyes when the desk stopped moving because he'd pushed it against the wall. The cat moved to sit on its ass and Damian stared at him.

"Go away. Shoo." The thing cocked his head at him as if he understood what he was saying. "Go away. There are monsters in this place that will eat you for dinner. Go away."

He was careful to keep his voice down, but the big cat roared loudly at him and he felt himself cringing back. And when the cat opened his mouth wide, Damian was sure he was going to snatch his head off. Instead, it was just a yawn. Then he laid down on the floor and stared at him. Damian looked at the size of the thing's paws and knew one swipe of it would tear his throat out.

"What are you doing here? Don't you know that I'm hiding, you moron? Go the fuck away." The low growl had him trying to get away from the creature, but he wasn't budging because he was blocked in by the desk and the cat.

When the cat put his mouth around his ankle and pulled, Damian screamed and tried to kick him away. When he let him go, Damian tried to get back under the desk. But the cat had other plans for him and grabbed his thigh this time. The bite was deep, the pain almost too much, but he didn't fight him this time. When he dragged him out from under the desk again, all he could do was hope that he wasn't going to be his dinner.

He was at the door when he was released this time. The cat looked at him then at the door. If he was thinking that Damian should open the fucker, then he was fucking stupid. Putting his hands under his ass, Damian shook his head and told him to go away.

The shift from beast to man was stunning. If he hadn't been so afraid, he might have asked him to do it again. But the big man that sat there naked shook his head, as if he knew what Damian was thinking. Instead of speaking, he reached up and opened the door, shoving Damian out of the way, then became a cat again. It all took less than a minute, and before he could think he should have run, the cat had his wrist in his mouth, this time pulling him down the hall to Peter's office.

No amount of pleading or begging could get the cat to let him go. He knew what was in that office. Dane and Peter. Whether or not his business partner was alive didn't really matter at this point; he was going to be killed and he had a feeling that it would not be an easy death. As soon as the cat ran his hand down the door, gouging out deep groves with his nails, the door opened and there she stood. His biggest fears were coming to light.

"Well there are you. Peter and I were beginning to think that you'd not be joining us. Good thing my mate here has such a good sense of smell. He was able to root you out because you smell of shit and fear. Did you mess your pants, Damian? Sure smells like it to me." Her laughter made his skin crawl. "Well, come on in and join the party. It'll be a blast now."

Damian knew what she was capable of. Not only had he seen her aftermath, but once he'd followed her to see her at work. Not that he didn't trust that she'd do a good job, but he was curious if she had help or not. He learned she didn't need

143

it.

Dane would kill effectively when it was called for. But she could make a person suffer in ways that made Damian sick. The only time he'd followed her, it had been the latter of the two. And she had made the man they had sent her after suffer more than he thought a person could and still be alive at the end.

She never cut into the man, nor did she use the guns that she had on her at all times. Just her fists and feet. The man, while bloodied, had begged for his life as Damian watched them, and at the end had pleaded for her to just kill him. Which she did, walking behind him and snapping his neck as if it was no more than a twig. He had never followed her or any of the other killers again. Once was more than enough for him.

"Come on now, have a seat." He looked up at her and opened his mouth to beg her as well. If that didn't work, he would give her money. More than he knew she could use in several lifetimes. "I don't want anything you have to offer me, Damian. I'm going to kill you, but I want answers first. How you reply...well, let's just say that you'll suffer less if you're truthful with me."

She jerked him up from the floor and slammed him into a chair. Then she taped his arms to the arm rests and his legs to the legs of it. He'd opened his mouth to tell her this was not right when she shoved a large piece of something metallic into his mouth. When she put her hand over his nose and mouth, he stared at her, unable to breathe.

"Swallow. Or you die right now." He shook his head. He had no idea what was in his mouth, but he sure as fuck wasn't going to obey. "Swallow it or I'll take it out of your mouth, cut your fucking gut open, and put it in you anyway. Fucking swallow."

In the end, he did. She had massaged his throat and

whispered in his ears all the things she was going to do to him. Fear. Terror. Whatever it was that he was feeling, it was going to be nothing, he knew, compared to how he felt when she was finished with him.

She sat on the desk, her legs swinging back and forth as she watched him. Damian wasn't going to live, so he decided right then that he was going to piss her off enough that she'd kill him quickly. When his brother found out about this, he'd hunt her down and kill her for him. He realized that he should have called him first thing when he realized that she was here. Damian looked around the room and noticed it was just him, her, and the big cat, who was headed to the bathroom that Peter had installed some weeks ago.

"Where is Peter?" She nodded to his left but he saw nothing. "Where? Have you killed him? Why are you doing this to us? We didn't do anything at all to you that you didn't sign off on. Let's just start over and you can go on doing what we wanted and we'll continue to pay you. It's simple really. Dane, you don't want to do this."

"Oh, but I do. And as for me signing off on something, do you mean like the *enhancement* drugs you gave me? I never signed on for those. You needed me for protection. I thought that's all I was. But you were drugging me so that I would do exactly what you wanted. You gave me those things so that I would be submissive to you, drugged to the point where I made no decisions on my own, but only the ones that you gave me." He wondered where she'd found that information, and decided that it mattered little right now. "Then if being submissive wasn't bad enough, you also had me running drugs for you. Or stealing them so that you could sell them. Nice little income you had there. All the glory and none of the issues. What did you plan to do if I was ever caught? Deny that as well?"

"Of course. And if my plan had worked the first time, you'd not be here at all. You should let me go. I failed in my attempt to kill you…that should mean something, don't you think?" He looked around and then back at her. "You were paid well for your part in this, Dane. Don't act like you didn't enjoy having all that cash to use as you wanted. What did you do with your part of the drug money? New car? A nice house? I bet you even got yourself some boy toy to play with too. You were just as guilty as we were."

"The money you gave me for working for you is just where it's been all along. In a savings account for all the victims' lives that you destroyed. Their families will be able to get some sort of comfort from this, at least. Oh, and it was nice of you and Peter to donate all that you had stashed away as well." He laughed. There was no way that she knew about his cash. "It was really generous of you to tell Peter about them. I know about the bank in the islands. The safe in your garage. Also, the three bank accounts that are in your dog's name. That was clever, by the way. I'd not have thought to look for those. But as you can imagine, Peter kept track of every single account that you opened. His too. Made it very easy for us to clean them out."

"No. No, that's not right. You can't do that to me." She asked him why not. "Because I worked hard for that money. You have no idea how much I had to put up with to make sure that I had a fallback plan if this went all to shit."

"It has gone to shit, Damian. And just so you know, you're not going to live long enough to spend it even if I didn't take it from you. You're as good as dead right now." The big naked man came in the room with her. This time he was clothed. When he sat down in the chair next to Dane, he tried to reason with him. His laughter made him think there was going to be no help from him either.

"You fucked up royally. And that's saying a lot considering what other shit we have to deal with on this. Why, just the things that Peter gave us is enough to get you both in prison for a long time. *If* it was in us to leave you alive." He asked again where Peter was. "Not something you should be worrying about. You need to be more concerned about what Dane has in mind for you."

"Please. You have to understand, this wasn't supposed to end this way. I never thought that you'd turn on us." She laughed at him. "You can't seriously think that this is right, Dane. We made you better than you were. That's a good thing, right?"

"No, it is not, you fucktard. I'm a killer. I have so many deaths on my head that if anyone were to look into it, they'd put me away forever." He said that he wouldn't tell. "You got that right. Because after today, you won't be around to tell anyone anything."

~~~

Brayden was worried about Dane. She was saying all the right things to this man, but her heart, he thought, wasn't into whatever it was they'd been asked to do. The other man, Peter, was locked in a room down the hall, and would remain there until they had the bank accounts that he claimed he had emptied. Christian was working on getting a judge to expedite things, and to get them a couple of warrants to close this place down as well. So, Dane was working to get a confession out of this man for the feds, who were listening in on the cameras that were set up around the room.

Dane really had started an account for the victims. Every check that she'd received from Nelson had been directly deposited in there each payday. The money under her bed, the money from the person who had hired her, she'd told him, was earned legally. Dane promised to explain when this was done.

Brayden reached out to his dad, trying to see what he knew so far. Brayden had been asked by Christian not to bother him yet, as he was trying to concentrate on the things going on around him. Namely the judge he was working with.

Nothing much moving around out here. I've seen a few cars slowing down to see what the hoopla is, though no one has been in or out of the estate but the police. He thanked him. *Brayden, do you think that young man is dead? The one that she went there to save?*

Yes, he's dead. His dad asked him if it had been quick. *No. It doesn't appear to have been. I don't know what Dane would have done had I not came by. When she asked me to come in, I thought for sure I was going to come up on a massacre. She was devastated at finding his body like that. When I found her, she was sitting in the hallway with a gun in her hand. I think she meant to kill them all, but something stopped her. She's broken up badly about all of this. I think she feels like a failure.*

Brayden had asked his brother to drive by the place, and they weren't even to it when he felt her pain. It was gut wrenching and so powerful that he had to have his brother pull over so he could get out of the car. He'd reached out to her then to ask if she was all right.

He's dead. David is dead. They murdered him before I got to save him. He told her he was sorry. *Not as sorry as these bastards are going to be when I'm finished with them. Brayden, I need you.*

He had no comment to her. Nothing at all. Her pain was so great that he could almost touch it himself. But he also knew something else. She was no longer a killer. That her heart had somehow changed when she'd met him. Or so he hoped. His dad interrupted his memories and he sat up higher in his seat.

Brayden, you're about to have some company. I can't see who it is right now, but they have an escort and they're heavily armed. Brayden asked if he could see who was in the vehicle. *No. But I don't think I'd want to be messing with these people. They're not even out of the cars yet and my cat is a little nervous. Who do you suppose it might be?*

Who knows with this group? Just be ready. If this is bad, then I don't want us here when they open fire on us. I think I'd like to die oblivious to it all. He wasn't sure if he was joking or not, but knew that whatever happened now was out of his hands. This had just taken on a whole new level of shit hitting the fan. He told Dane.

Thanks. I wondered when he'd get here. He started to ask if she knew him when she smiled at Damian. "You are so fucked right now. Your brother is on his way in."

"No. No, you can't have.... What brother? I don't have a brother at all." Dane said nothing and honestly, Brayden was speechless too. She knew these people? "What have you done, Dane? This will not end well for me. How could you do this to me? Your friend."

"You're not my friend and you fucking know it. And I didn't call him. Davie did before you brought him here. I would have but...well, you fucked up those plans, didn't you, moron?" He asked her how she knew. "It was easy, really. After a couple of trips through your trash can on your email server, it was fairly easy to figure out that you'd been warned, several times, about your activities. He's not a happy camper. I'm pretty sure that you're going to never see the light of day again. And when I contacted him over you, guess what? He hired me to watch you until he could figure out what to do with your sorry ass."

"Kill me." She laughed and stood up. "Please. You have no idea what sort of things he can do to me. He has connections. Damn it, Dane, you've really fucked me over with this. How

149

could you?"

"Easy." She went to the window and stared out. While Brayden wanted to join her, he was still in a state of shock. She had called someone in to help her with this? And whoever it was, they were related to the piece of shit right here? This needed some thought. His dad warned him that they were coming in hot. Armed, in other words.

Ten big men came in first. They were large in every sense of the word too. Rifles in their hands, guns at their hips, as well as a couple had them sticking out of the top of their pants. They were making no bones about showing off the fact that they were ready. Brayden watched them as they surrounded Damian.

Brayden didn't move when one of them put a gun behind his head. He put out his hands so that they could see that he was unarmed and sat still. When another approached Dane, she smiled at him and told him if he touched her, it would be the last time he moved. He must have known she wasn't kidding because the guy backed away from her.

A well-dressed man came in next. Brayden wouldn't have had to guess the two men were related. They looked enough alike to perhaps be twins. Yet the other man was older than Damian by a few years. And this man wasn't happy. More than that, he looked as if he was going to take it out on Dane rather than his brother. As he watched him approach his mate, his cat got pissy quickly. It was all he could do not to let him protect her when the man looked over at him. A wink and a smile from the man didn't make him feel good about any of this right now.

"Let him go. He's not the one you should be keeping an eye on." The man looked back at Dane as he continued. "You should have told me yourself. It almost took me too long to figure out who was calling me."

"I've been busy. And you told me that the next time I called you, I'd better be willing to do something for you. I think I did that." Dane moved to stand with him. "His family is outside right now. Can they come in? I think they're about as curious as you are."

"Of course. Brayden, is it?" He nodded. "Do call in your family. I'm anxious to meet them. And that mother of yours. I've heard great things about her."

Brayden was confused but he did as he was asked. His dad came in first, then his brothers, all of them in various stages of dress. His mom was the last to enter, looking as beautiful as he'd ever seen her. When she stood before the man still standing by the window, she did the most incredible thing. She slapped him.

No one moved. Not the men that were armed well enough to take on an army, nor the man she'd hit. And when he suddenly stared to laugh, Brayden looked at Dane. She hadn't expected that either, if the look on her face was any indication.

"That's for not coming here sooner and taking care of this mess. You knew what he was, and now two very good friends of my future daughter-in-law are dead. Shame on you." The man sobered quickly. "What were you thinking? Or were you?"

"No. I was not. And to be honest with you, I had no idea this was going on until about a month ago. But I was told to stand down until I heard from Dane." He looked over at her as he continued to talk to his mom. "My name is Walter Sams, brother to this fool here. But since Dane disappeared it's been everything I could do not to come here and figure out what had happened to her. She's not just someone that works for me, but a good friend as well. However, she did assure me before this that she had it under control and should I step in, I'd be in the middle of it. I trusted her. And for good reason."

"Then I apologize." Walter told his mom that there was no

151

need for that. He was sorry. "She's come to mean a great deal to me and my family. You can understand how, with her being hurt as she has been, we'd take it personally."

"Yes. And she means a great deal to mine as well. I'd not have one if not for her." Brayden wanted to ask, but he was cut off when Damian started talking. He wanted his brother to cut him loose.

"Walter, I want you to make her let me go. This has been a complete misunderstanding on her part. And she's a thief. I don't know if you're aware of that, but she took all my money. Peter's too, but he's on his own." Damian looked around. "Well? Someone cut me loose. I would like to get out of here before the police show up and make it impossible for me to get out in one piece. And she made me swallow something. I think it's a tracker. Whatever you do, don't let anyone get into the program so I don't die. You'd not like that, would you, Walter?"

"You're not going anywhere, you fuck face. You're going to pay for your crimes. And as for what I made you swallow, it was a marble, nothing like you put into those poor people that you experimented on. I hope it plugs you up so tightly that you have to have your ass cut open so you can take a shit. Had it not been for Dr. Stanton, I'm sure you would have figured out a way to kill me off as well when you realized that your previous plan to kill me failed." Damian looked at Dane when she spoke again. "This mess here is the least of your problems, Walter. He's been dipping into your company money too. Murder. Robbery. Kidnapping. Attempted—"

"You cannot still be trying to get me into hot water over that thing with the kids, are you? For heaven's sake, I didn't make it work, so that isn't my fault. You were in the way then as well, but I let you live." Brayden asked what had happened. "She thwarted my plans to take Walter's children on a little trip.

I would have brought them right back after he paid me, but she got in the way. Damn it, Dane. You're a problem that should have been dealt with a long time ago. I don't know what went wrong when you were supposed to be dead this time either."

"I was taken in by a very nice family; the word nice, in case you don't know the meaning of it, is the opposite of what you are." Dane grinned at Brayden. "You are the best thing that's happened to me. I'm so glad that your brother found me when he did."

Kissing her on the nose, he held her to him as Walter talked to his brother. It was surreal, really. Brayden knew who he was, even if his family might not. He was a part of the mob, a large part of it according to the articles that he'd read. And Damian, he thought, was worse than any criminal that he'd ever heard of as well. To think his mom had slapped him, and now he was talking to his parents like they'd been friends forever. Yes, this was going to go down as one of the oddest days of his life.

Soon after they were asked to leave, except for Dane, who was asked to hang out for a little while longer. He had no doubt that Damian was going to be taken care of. Brayden did wonder about Peter. But as they were making their way down the hall to the outside of the lab, he saw more security gathering him up and dragging him down to the office they had just left. What he wouldn't give to be in that room for this.

Brayden was still waiting in the yard when the local police showed up. The feds had been there almost from the start, but no one was doing much more than waiting. The locals were asked to wait by the people that had come to protect Walter. Brayden could see that was pissing them off, but Sams's people standing outside the lab weren't budging. Brayden thought it was somewhat funny that the locals thought that just because it was their town they should be involved. Sams being a large man with an army behind him sort of trumped their local jurisdiction, he was pretty sure.

CHAPTER 11

Dane wasn't ready to go in the house just yet, so she made her way to the deck out back and sat there. Too much. Everything that had happened was just too much to deal with. And when someone cleared their throat, she nodded at Denny and told him to have a seat.

"You know a war lord." Nodding, she told him she'd known him for a long time. "I see. And you helped him by saving his family too."

"Yes. Damian had it in his head to kidnap his brother's children to get him to sign off on some kind of deal he was working on. I guess sign off is the wrong term. He wanted him to give him money to start up some sort of madness that he was forever dreaming up." Dane looked at Denny. "You should know that though I've been working for Walter for a very long time, I don't have anything to do with his businesses. It was more that I was taking care of a few things that were illegal in a few police stations, as well as his brother. I've known him about ten years now, around the time he became a made-man."

Denny rocked in the swing but didn't speak. She wasn't one to fill in the silences either, so they just rocked and said nothing. She could almost feel the thousand and one questions that were circling in his head, but he was quiet about them. Brayden was a great deal like his father in that. They would think out a problem rather than babble on about it.

"This man, Damian, you were reporting to this Walter person on what he was doing?" Dane told him she had, and that was why she'd been able to let him know when to come here. "He tried to hurt his kids. Is there a reason that he didn't do anything about his brother then?"

"Yes." If he expected her to elaborate, he didn't say anything. She wasn't at liberty to tell anyone what had happened that day. About how not only had Damian tried to take the kids, but he'd harmed Walter, as well as his wife. They didn't want it known how he'd slipped by the security and nearly killed his wife. It was touch and go for a while with Nita. And that was when Dane had gone to Walter and asked if she could take care of it.

"I was enhanced while I was undercover for the lab, trying to get information on what it was they were doing. It wasn't anything that I had planned on, but it was the only way I could get the information that was needed to bring them all down. Peter Nelson started out being a good guy in the wrong place, but soon he showed his true colors and became as bad as Damian. But then I was found out. I don't think it was Damian, but it could have been. He or both he and Peter had hired someone to take me out of the equation. That was when I lost my memory of everything." Denny nodded, but again, he didn't comment. "I'm sorry about all this."

"Sorry? Why? I mean, it's not like you planned on any of this to happen. And as far as I can see, even hurt as you were, you tried your best to make things right. I hate to think what might have happened to you should that man have done what he'd set out to do. And to his own family too." She'd be dead, that's what would have happened to her. "Dane, are you still working for Walter Sams? I mean, even after this, will you still be there for him?"

"Yes, but again, not in a capacity that has anything to do with his line of work. Even thugs need things to be legal, don't you think? Besides, if you've been reading up on Walter, you'll see that he's trying to make things right. And if it would make you feel any better about him, he'd come and talk to you." He nodded but didn't ask in what capacity she meant, nor did he tell her that she shouldn't. "I have to talk to Brayden about it. I'm not sure how he's going to feel about me being gone for long periods of time to do things for Walter."

"I would imagine that he'd be very proud of you. Not to mention, he more than likely would love to be by your side. I'm not sure how I'll feel about that. Let's face it, child, he's a good man, but not a fighter." She laughed as he stood up. "I should be going on in now. I know that Brayden needs to talk to you about a couple of things anyway. Oh, and congratulations on the new home. I'm certainly glad you're going to have it close enough so that when you are home, we can visit when we want."

"Home?"

Denny was still laughing when he went into the house. Following him, she knew, wouldn't give her any more answers, but she did think he was a sneaky man. When Brayden came out of the house a few minutes later, she wondered if he'd been sent by Denny and decided it didn't matter. She was glad to see him.

"How are you doing?" She told him she was overwhelmed a little, but all right. "Yeah, right there with you on that one. When I saw Walter Sams enter that room, I.... Well, couldn't have seen that one coming. I thought for sure that we were all dead."

"I forgot I knew him. But he's not as bad as the papers put

157

him out to be." He nodded, then laughed. She supposed it was funny in a way. "I'm sorry. I would have told you, but I wasn't sure he was coming. I mean, he told me to call him, but I had Davie do it. I just wasn't sure he'd believe a stranger over me. He has trust issues, as you can well imagine."

"Yes, I can understand that. A man in his position, he'd have to know who to trust and not to. Those men, they made him some major trouble, I'm guessing. A name like Sams, it can either close a lot of doors or open them. Do you know what happened to those two? Or what will happen to them?" She nodded. "Can't tell me, huh? Okay. I think there will be times when you can't tell me everything. And I think I can handle that. So long as I know that you're being safe."

"Always. Especially now with you in my life." He picked her up and sat her on his lap. She noticed that Denny did the same to Lucy when he was nervous about something or thinking hard about a problem. It was as if they needed the comfort for decisions that they didn't care for. "If it's all right with you, I'm going to be doing jobs for him. I won't be able to tell you about them, as you've guessed, but there might be times when I have to leave for a bit. I won't have any contact with you during that time. It's dangerous, but the pay is good and I like it. So long as I'm not dealt a shitty hand."

"I don't have to like it, but I do understand. I don't know how well I'll do about you being gone for periods of time either, but we'll get through it, correct?" He held her, rocking slowly back and forth in the big outdoor recliner he was sitting in. "I've been thinking about a couple of things. Oh, and I've been briefed on a few subjects, like how I can't talk about Sams or any kind of conversations that you might have with him. And I guess our home is not up to standard for what you're doing. A team is going over it and putting in security far better than what I would have done. Is this legal? I mean, are you going to get into trouble working for a mob boss?"

"No. And this is just between you and me. Walter is working with the government, and in turn, so am I. He has been working for them for a while now. It's one of the reasons that he's been trying to turn over a new leaf, to show others that someone can go straight and not have to murder and steal for profit. As for the security, that's not just him but part of the program he's working for. Your family's homes will be done too. We have to keep them safe so that they can't be used against us. Speaking of which, we own a house?" He nodded, but still looked worried. Not that she blamed him. "I could quit. I mean, he told me that I could just hang up my gloves so to speak and not work for him."

"You'd not like that anymore than I would if someone asked me not to work on projects. It's in your blood. You need to do it as much as I need for you to be happy and safe." She asked him what he'd been thinking about. "Oh. I'd like for you to get me trained. Not just on how to use a gun...I think that's important, but hand to hand combat training as well. There might be times when my cat won't be able to come to the rescue. Not to mention, I'd very much like to be able to defend your honor if it ever comes to that."

"I can arrange that. Julian asked me the same thing. Do you think your other brothers would want some training as well?" He told her that he thought they could all use it. "I know a couple of people that you can work with. One of them I trained, and she now trains the president's agents on how to use their bodies efficiently. I'll look into that for you all. What else is bothering you?"

"The second thing. I want you to marry me. I know that I should be down on one knee in front of you, begging you to make an honest man of me, but to be truthful, I'm a little fearful that you're not a proposal sort of person. You might just kick me in the head or something." They both laughed. "I love you, Dane. Very much so. And if you could see your way to marrying me, I'd be about as happy as a man could be."

"There will be times when I'm afraid that you might not love me." He told her that was never going to happen. "I'll be shot at. Sometimes I'll be hurt. There will be times when—"

He put his hand over her mouth. "If it's all the same to you, I'd rather not know what you might have happen to you, and focus more on the question at hand. Will you marry me, please?"

Removing his hand, she kissed it before holding it with her own. "I'm afraid, if I'm honest with you. And I want to be, all the time. I don't want you hurt, and there will be people out there that will know that they can get to me by harming you guys. It would devastate me if that happened."

"We're family. No matter what happens, we'll always be here for you and you for us." She nodded and stood up near the deck railing. "Would you like to go and see the house? I'm sorry about buying it without you looking at it first. But I had to do something or go nuts. Or nuttier."

"Yes, I'd love to see it."

Before they left, Denny came back out on the deck. Apparently, Patrick was there to see Brayden. They sat down at his parents' dining room table and Patrick handed them a thick file. Brayden passed it to Dane when she asked and she looked through it as the man spoke.

~~~

"I want to start by saying that none of what I'm about to tell you will come out in the papers here. And your name has been taken off the files, both here and at home. As far as I'm

160

concerned, you were never involved in any of this, and there is no reason to bring your name into a mess that can be solved by you helping me. Or some of it anyway. No one, not unless you tell them, will associate you with Vonda Hull." Brayden nodded. "Also, because you've helped us solve this case, you will receive the reward that was put forth for that help."

"I'd rather you didn't do that. I don't need the money, and I'm sure that it can go for something else." Patrick told him it was done. Brayden looked over at Dane when she cleared her throat. "What do you think?"

"That the money should go for something good. A way for it to make a difference in someone's life." He nodded and looked back at Patrick. "You said that Brayden wouldn't be mentioned. Why are you doing that? I mean, other than the obvious reasons that he didn't have anything to do with it. I'm sure that there are people out there who know he was involved with this other woman. How will you keep him out of that?"

"So long as neither he nor anyone else mentions it, as I said, then no one will connect him to her. And while we're running that, we'll run an article that talks about Brayden's charity work, donations that he's made, as well as his help in making sure that the good citizens are safe and have a place to call their own. They'll remember the bad things more, but without his name there, it will lessen the impact. We hope. Speaking of the project, it's what brings me to the second thing. Project Housing, the one that you were working with back home. You were there when things started to go to hell in a handbasket. I need whatever information you can give me regarding who was in charge. Who was the person who made work assignments, as well as anything you know about the material donations?" Brayden told him he'd be glad to give him whatever he had. Excusing himself, he made his way to his computer.

He was just coming into the room again when he heard Dane laughing. He wondered what it was about when he entered the room and saw that she had pinned Patrick to the floor by holding one hand behind his back, nearly to his neck.

"Dane?" She let the detective go and moved back to her seat. They were both laughing, so he figured there wasn't any reason for panic. "Do I even want to know what's going on?"

"I asked her to show me how she made that move...the one where she took down that perp that I read about in the reports." Brayden wondered about it but Patrick elaborated. "I found some files about the two of you on my desk this morning that I was interested in. Someone sent them over to me. The note on the top said that if I made her upset, it made him upset, and that wouldn't be a good thing. I agree with him. Even where I live, Walter Sams carries a great deal of weight when he needs something done."

"I've seen her in action, but not a lot. She's very good with a gun, I'm to understand, and she can take on someone twice her size without much effort." Patrick said he'd like to see that sometime. "She's going to be training us, the family. I think that's a good thing as well."

"I do too. No one can be prepared enough when it comes to fools that want to harm you. I have drills at my house for fires and such. Too many simple things can go wrong if you don't have just a little bit of training on something." Brayden asked him where he was from originally. "Texas, believe it or not. When the opportunity came up for us to have a good job and some perks, we loaded up and moved. Best decision I've ever made."

Brayden brought up on his computer what he had and showed it to the man. He asked questions, mostly names and addresses if he had them. Then he requested a copy of the receipts he had.

"Why? I don't understand what my personal receipts have to do with this." He smiled. "I'll give them to you, but I would like to know why."

"Of course, and I'll tell you. You keep receipts for everything, correct? Even the cash items?" Brayden said that he did, Christian had asked him to do that. "That's why I need them. It will go to show how organized you are. How much you spent of your own money, and where it went. This man, the one you said was in charge, he's saying that you were forever forgetting to give him the receipts on such items like drywall and other items, and then would make up a number well above what they thought it should have cost. I'm sure that they're all lying, but I need some sort of proof and this will do it. You're a very well respected man, Brayden, and I'm terribly sorry this is happening to you."

"Thank you. That's very good to know. But I was never in charge of those things." Patrick said he knew that as well. "You think to catch him in his own lies? I know that there were times when I thought there should have been more material to work with, and when I mentioned it, the next day there would be plenty. I thought at first that it was just a matter of storage. But towards the end, I knew there was a major problem."

"Yes, we've come to find out there was a lot of cash changing hands all over the place. And drugs as well. It's terrible when you can't even trust a charity. But as for the men, we hope to catch them with the cash. Just over fifty million dollars is missing from the accounts for this organization. And on top of that, there are truckloads of water, food, as well as materials to build with that haven't been accounted for either. One of the men who was supposed to oversee the daily count of these things came up missing just before I left there. I recently heard from one of my own that he was caught trying to leave the country with about four million in cash. His house was raided about an hour ago, and the things we found there put a large dent in what has been claimed as missing." Brayden had known something was going on. What it was he had no idea, but there had been some critical problems on the job. "With your help, we hope to bring in the rest of them."

"I'll do what I can. But as I told you before, I had little to nothing to do with the funding of the project. It wasn't until someone put my name on some of the billing that I got concerned enough to leave there." He said he understood that. "What is it you're hoping to gain with this? I mean, most of the money is returned. The project is still underway. I doubt that anyone will find it all."

"You're right, we won't. But I do want to make sure that people will think twice about trying to harm a nice charity like this again. We lost a lot of credit with the way this thing went. And I for one would hate to think that people who need it the most are the ones that will suffer. We need help, and without funding like this, they'll never get it." Brayden said that he was sure that they'd get it back. "I just want to make sure that once we are in the black again, we stay there. This is a good thing you people were doing. I'd like for it to continue. And it won't if we can't show that we're doing everything in our power to make sure that it does."

After giving him copies of all the information that he had, including receipts, they made their way home. His car was at the other house, and the plan was to walk over then drive back. Brayden had things to do in the morning, and he didn't want to be without his car if either of them needed it. Holding Dane's hand, he told her what he knew about the house.

"It's large. Bigger than I first thought about buying. But I hope that someday we can fill it with children if you'd like." She told him that was fine. He knew that she was distracted and he knew that he was adding to her stress level. "We could get a couple of goats too if you want. That way I don't have to mow the lawn."

"That's nice. Do you think Patrick will find the rest of the money? I mean, all of it?" Brayden said that he wasn't sure but he seemed to be trying. "I can find it. It's what I do."

"You should ask if you can help him. Maybe he could use your extra eyes to find it." She said that she would first thing. "Now, are you ready to see our new house? It looks like we're being updated now."

There were men everywhere. On the grounds and the garage. There were even a couple of them on the roof. Dane talked to some of them, asking if they were keeping up on training as they entered the house. A few more of the men and women spoke to her as well while they worked. All of them, it seemed, knew her and liked her. Dane introduced him to everyone.

"Hello. You must be Doctor and Mrs. Stanton." Brayden nodded and Dane smiled at the man that was wearing a nice suit. Brayden had rarely been referred to with that title where it had given him so much pride. "My name is Tillman. I'm going to be working the household for the two of you. Walter Sams said that he would talk to you later regarding my duties."

"He told us that someone he trusted would be in the house." Tillman said that would be him. Brayden looked around at the other people, all dressed in a livery. "I'm assuming that these folks will be here as well?"

"Only if you approve. There will be a need for them to be in place for functions, but otherwise, they'll work the house under my supervision. They've all been handpicked by me, and I'm to oversee making sure that they're toeing the line as well. We don't wish anything to happen to the family."

"Why are they dressed like they're working for a large plantation?" He felt his face heat up when Dane spoke. "I mean, is it necessary that they all dress the same?"

"It is, my lady. This way when someone comes into the household, you'll know immediately if they are working here or are unwanted trouble. Their uniforms will change periodically, and you will be given advance notice of the colors they'll wear. That should thrall someone trying to slip past the other security measures in place. Each person here has a name badge that will get them in and out of the house, as well as tell us where they are should there be an issue. Each person here, even the workers, are all bonded by the state as well as have clearance." Brayden wondered at that but didn't comment. "The upper floors have been completed. The household storage area has been given a boost as well. The office will have monitors put in before they leave today, as well as a security system that will be off the grid."

"I'm sorry. What?" Tillman looked at him and asked what he meant. "I don't know anything that you're talking about. I don't mean to sound stupid, but could you explain to me what you're saying in laymen's terms? I'm new to this whole major security thing."

"Of course, my lord. Your staff is well trained to help should someone try to enter the house without permission. Also, their name badges are electronically enhanced so that they will use them to get in and out of the household. No one, under any circumstances, will be let in by someone in the house. The upper floors have a different code on them so that only a select few can go up there. You and the missus will have your own code…not a badge, but a keypad. If that is satisfactory to you."

Brayden said that it was. "Very good. A monitor system with cameras and voice activation is connected to the computer that is in the office on the upper floors. This will be monitored here and offsite in the event that there is an emergency and power is cut off at the home."

"So much security. Are you sure that's necessary?" Instead of answering, Tillman nodded once and walked away. Brayden looked at Dane. "What's going on?"

"It's necessary. The security, the cameras. Even the people here. When I work, you'll be here all alone. And I'm not saying that you can't protect yourself, but you won't be able to protect everyone, and that would include the children you wish to have with me, your family, as well as anyone that might come here to visit." He asked her if she thought that would be a problem. "Yes. There will be times when I'm on an assignment and you'll be with me. Someone has to be here to make sure that your family is safe and sound too."

"Okay. I get it. I guess in a way I didn't think this was going to be an issue. I can see now that it's a lot more complicated than I thought."

She wandered ahead of him into the main part of the house. He looked at things with new eyes, those of someone that might mean to harm them.

Hazards of all kinds were everywhere, he could see now. The big windows in the front of the house gave them a clear view of the driveway, but anyone coming up could see in as well. There were doors on each side of the house. More ways for someone to enter. The smaller windows through this part of the house were just low enough that someone could come in by just breaking the glass. He made his way into the living room, where Dane was talking to a man dressed in camo, and went to them. It was high time he took a serious interest in his safety.

167

"Perry, this is my mate, Brayden Stanton. Brayden, this is Perry LaRue. He is one of the people that you're going to be working with. His sister, Allie, will be joining us to help as well. Perry specializes in weaponry and Allie in hand to hand. And don't be fooled by her size. She can pack a hell of a hit when she wants." Brayden shook the other man's hand and told him he was glad to be working with him. "He's going to come back in the morning to start on things with you and the others. I told him we were having our home gone over, and he's going to have a look at it as well."

Taking her hand, they made their way to the uppermost floors. He thought it would be the best way to go, from the top down, then to his parents' house. The house was a great deal larger than he'd thought and pictures didn't do it justice.

CHAPTER 12

The third floor of the house had once been the servant's quarters, with three bathrooms as well as five bedrooms. The crew in this part of the house was now changing some of the spaces to safe rooms for the family, as well as updating two for the staff that would be on site all the time. A common kitchen area was going to be updated as well. Dane looked around and was glad that they were being enlarged. Some of them had been no bigger than her closet at home.

"I'm guessing that Tillman will be up here." She said that he was going to be in the basement. "Oh. Why?"

"He asked and I saw no reason for him to not take it. If you'd rather him be up here, I can tell him. He's pretty easy." Brayden told her that was fine with him too. "He's a very solitary man. He's friendly but prefers his own company to having anyone around. I'm sort of like that too, but I enjoy being with you."

"Good save." They both laughed as they made their way down the narrow stairs to the second floor. "The master suite is on the left, I was told, and five bedrooms on the right. Want to start with the five first?"

They wandered through the bedrooms. All of them were a good size and very well maintained. There were two shared bathrooms for two of the bedrooms each, and one that was in the hallway. Dane liked that they had large walk-in closets. She

169

told him about how she'd lived in a one room flat once that had no closet.

"Everything I owned was in baskets. I didn't have a lot, mind you, but enough that it was annoying as fuck to try and get dressed in the morning. I think that this will be fun for whoever takes these rooms." She led the way to the master suite. "Christ, this is huge."

The room was large, with room for a king-sized bed, several dressers, as well as two large closets that were hidden behind oak doors. Inside them were built in dressers, plus a shoe rack for them both. She marveled at the tie rack that rotated when a button was pressed. She wondered what he would look like in a suit and tie, and decided it was just too much for her heart. He looked good in anything, but she liked him best when he wore nothing at all. Dane walked into the bathroom when Brayden called her name.

"We could both shower in here and never touch each other." He pulled her into his arms as he stood in the empty stall. "I'm thinking that I'll enjoy this. As much as I will the big bed when it comes in. We'll have to order all kinds of things to fill this place up."

"I have some things in storage. Not a great deal. The bed I have is small so I know that's not going to be of any use to us. You're very possessive of the bed." He swatted her on the ass and she rolled her groin into his hardening cock. "We're not alone here. I counted about fifty people just inside the house. There's more than likely that many more outside."

"We'll have to be really quiet then." He picked her up and Dane wrapped her legs around his hips. "If I take you against the wall, what do you think the chances are there are cameras to see us?"

"Probably not hooked up just yet. And even if they were,

I'm pretty sure that no one will see them after I go and find them. We don't want anyone to get the wrong impression about us, now do we?" He took her to the counter and sat her on the edge of it. She was wet already, and he'd not even touched her yet. "Brayden, you're making me crazy."

"Honey, you've been driving me insane all day. I cannot wait to see you naked." She helped him undress her. Their clothing wasn't going to last long at this rate, and she laughed when she heard his buttons pinging all over the floor. Finally, he put his hands on either side of her blouse and ripped it off her. "I need you."

Brayden barely got his pants down around his thighs before he was filling her. Dane cried out with the first of what she hoped would be many releases. Her body was primed for his. And when he started fucking her, taking her hard where she sat, Dane came three more times, hard releases that didn't give her what she needed. More, was all she could think...she needed more.

Picking her up, he took her to the wall in the bathroom. The rest of her clothing, rags really, were torn away. Her breasts were aching for his touch. And when he took her into his mouth, sucking hard, she held him to her, curling her fingers in his hair as she gave him all she had.

"Come for me." She cried out when he commanded her. But her body wasn't ready yet...she needed him, something only he could give her. "Come for me, love. I need to feel you tighten around me. Milking my cock with your sheath."

"Bite me." He growled low, making her hum with it. "Brayden, please. Bite me so that I can come with you."

It wasn't just a bite but a tearing of the flesh at her shoulder. She screamed loudly, not caring if the household heard them. And when he suckled at the wound, drinking her down, she

171

came again. Her body felt as if it had been snapped like a rubber band before the next climax took her over the edge.

Stars. She saw stars of every color behind her eyelids. There were sparkles of light. Tremors shook her to the core. Even as she came again and again, it was as if she was being rung out, hung upside down and then shaken up again. She wasn't sure if she could take much more. It was too much; her body was done. Then Brayden came, bringing her again as he filled her body with his. In seconds her body went limp and her mind joined it.

When she woke, she was lying on the floor. His shirt, or what was left of it, was covering her, but she wasn't worried. Stretching the kinks out of her back from being on the floor, she stood up and saw the duffle bag near the bathroom door. Going to it, she read the note that had her name on it.

Darling, I'm sorry about the clothes. (Well, not really. That was spectacular.) We'll have to move in fast so we don't have to be naked when we have company. But here is a bag of my things. Find something and come on down. I think you're going to be happy with what I've been up to. He then signed it, Love, Brayden.

Finding a pair of his boxers and a large tee shirt to pull on had her digging through the rest of his things to find a pair of socks too. Her bra was destroyed, as were her panties, but she was happy, and she figured there were worse things that could be happening right now. Going down the stairs, she found him in the office with Christian.

"We were just talking about you." She started to sit down on the box that hadn't been in the room before when she noticed that there was a pair of chairs, as well as some rugs that were rolled up in the corner. "I had a few things in storage and Christian was kind enough to bring them over. I owe him dinner."

"Great. As soon as I figure out something to wear besides your things, we'll go. I'm starved." She loved the way their faces turned a nice shade of pink and laughed at them both. "You guys always this destructive with clothing or is it just mates?"

"I wouldn't know. And I more than likely won't, either." She asked Christian why. "Because I'm an attorney. And you've heard that we're the scum of the earth. Anyway, I have some other things in the truck, and Mom and Dad are coming over later with more furniture that you had in storage at their home."

"I need something to put on." Brayden looked her over then wiggled his brows at her. "Something that is a little more covering and less revealing. You dork. I doubt very much that your parents would appreciate having a look upstairs either. I think we broke the counter."

They hadn't, but it was funny to see Brayden jump up and look around. Christian was still laughing when he told her he needed her signature on a few things. Mostly accounts that Brayden had already established. As she put her name where he told her, she asked him about her money.

"The cash that was picked up for you is in a safe in the basement of my house. I can bring it to you whenever you want. The guns are in storage as well. I would suggest that you get a nice sized gun safe to put them in, as well as one for this house for cash. I'm assuming you always get paid in cash, right?" She told him for the most part, yes. "All right then. A big safe. I can look into that for you and have one delivered if you want."

"That would be nice of you. Also, I have some accounts as well. Bank, as well as a few credit cards. I don't use them much, but I have them. Additionally, I have two houses, one here and another in Europe. Both are inheritances from my family. Can you put Brayden's name on those as well?" He told her it would be his pleasure. "I'd like to talk to you about something important when you have time."

"I do now. Or is it private?" She said that now was fine. "All right then. I have to ask, is it legal? If so, then I'd like for you to answer a question for me as well, if you can."

"I can answer whatever you want. You might not like the answers, but I will be truthful." He nodded. "Me first. The work I do, it's not for a mobster. I can't tell you a great many details, but I can tell you that much. I don't want you to think that I'm doing things that would harm this family."

"I didn't. Walter had a long talk with the family before he left. We are all aware of your working relationship. And we'll take that to the grave." She figured that Walter would have talked to them, but she wasn't always sure about the man. "Is that what you wanted me to know?"

"Yes. I like you. All of you, and I don't want any of you to think that I'm a terrible person. It's important to me to keep you safe, but I would really hate that you can't trust me for what I do." He thanked her. "Now, what is it you wanted to tell me?"

"Right. I'd like for you to let me help you when I can." She asked him why. "Why? Okay, good question. I have it in my head to run for a few political jobs. That's not all of it, but some. I also would feel better knowing that you're not brought in on something you can't get out of. I can guide you, legally that is, if you want to use that word, in some things that might feel off for you."

"I'd like that. Thank you." He nodded. "I need to get a few things out of my old place, now that I know where it is. Also...I had a cell phone when I was hurt. I know where it is now. I was wondering if you could somehow get it to someone that can use it. Not Walter. He needs to deal with stuff on his own with Damian, but there are things on the phone that might help a few others."

"Like how?" Dane told him. "You mean closure for a few unsolved deaths. I can do that. I'd worry about it coming back on you. Do you think it will?"

"Not if you do it right, it won't." They were laughing when Brayden came back down the stairs with a large trash can. She could see shards of glass in it, as well as some of her things that had once been a pretty shirt. They were headed to the car when she told Christian where the phone was. "The warehouse that I was found by, the second floor has an office. In it is a stuffed chair. The phone is in the cushion under the seat."

"I'll make sure that it gets into the right hands." She assured him that she trusted him with it. "Thank you. I'll see you guys later."

~~~

The house was starting to fill out. There were still a lot of things that they needed, mostly pictures and some personal touches, but all in all, Brayden was happy with it. He was just going into his office when Tillman came out of the kitchen. He looked upset.

"Anything I can do to help?" The man shook his head then nodded. "Tell me whatever it is and we'll work it out. I'm in a great mood today and feel I can take on the world."

"It isn't that much, my lord, but just some updating. The kitchen is.... How should I say this? It's subpar. The refrigerator is nearly on its last legs. There is not enough hot water to wash the dishes and to clean. I think that the hot water heater is very old as well. And you should know that the pantry is not nearly big enough for when you entertain. I'm to understand that you have a very large family." He told him he had five brothers and his parents. "That alone will make the pantry strain at the sides. I would like to suggest you have someone come in and renovate things so that they are at least up to this decade."

"I know very little about updating anything, but I'm sure you have a better idea of what we need than I would. How about you get whoever you can trust and bring it all the way to this year? I don't want to have to worry about food or cleaning when there are other things out there." Tillman started to walk away but turned back. "Something else?"

"Yes. I have hired a guard for the front gate. It's being put in now, so when it is finished, you'll have someone out there at all times." He thanked him. "Sir, I must say that I'm very happy to be working with you. You have a good head on your shoulders and are not afraid to ask for help when it is necessary. Thank you."

"Thank you, Tillman. You've made this so much easier on both Dane and I than I think we realize. We have a good staff. People working the grounds that can keep us safe. I don't think a man could ask for a better person in the position than you."

Tillman walked away without saying anything, but Brayden noticed that he was a little taller looking. Going into his office, he sat at his desk and began answering emails. It was going to be a long afternoon as this rate.

Over an hour later, he came to the third email from a man that he'd dealt with earlier in the month. He had asked him to come in and evaluate his firm for any kind of problems. It wasn't what he did and he'd tried to explain that to the man, but he was insistent so Brayden read over all the emails again.

He was no closer to figuring out what to do when Dane came into the room. He told her all about the man, his business as well as what he wanted. She said that was something she could do while she wasn't working with Walter.

"You'd not mind?" Dane told him no, she was bored. "I bet this is a little slower than you're used to. Oh, and I met Allie this morning. She's tough as nails, isn't she? I mean, she might have you beat in that department."

"She is. And only human too. She knows about shifters, but per her brother, she's not had a lot of time dealing with any. I guess she's kind of nervous working with you guys. Not that you'd hurt her, but simply because of the unknown factor." Brayden said that she'd told him pretty much the same thing. "How did it go? I mean, you look like you survived it."

"I might need you to give me a nice rubdown later." He wiggled his brows at her and she laughed. "I love you, Dane. Very much."

"And I love you too. And if you play your cards right, I might give your entire body a rubdown." He asked her about right now. "Your parents are coming over. Something about some store fronts that they want you to consider. And Levi is here now. He has it in his head that we need to let him paint a mural on the nursery wall. I tried to explain to him we don't have kids yet, but he's set on it."

He followed her out of the office. Whatever he didn't get done, he knew it would be there tomorrow. Or even the next day. This was what he'd missed being gone for so long. Family. And he was glad to have them all home and safe.

His parents were in the newly furnished living room. There were three large couches, two chairs, and several stands that held lamps. No television was in this room, and he wasn't sure that they'd even get one for in here. But the room was cozy despite its size, and bright with light from the big doors. He couldn't wait to see it all decorated for Christmas. After hugging them both, he sat with Dane on the couch.

"Son, I was thinking we should plan a project together. You and me. I have an idea where we could raise a bit of cash and have a nice town get together." He asked his dad when he wanted to do this. "Well, it's coming up on the Fourth. What

177

do you think about putting it out there that we want to have an old fashion street fair? People can sell some things, bake a few desserts, and maybe we could get something to put on that big spit that we had put in the park a few years back."

"You mean get a hog and roast it?" Dad said that was what he was thinking, yes. "I like that idea, but it's only about three weeks away. Do you think we can get the town behind us so quickly?"

"I think we can. And if we have to put in a little of our own this year, we could try and make it a yearly thing. I think this town could use a little fun, don't you? I mean, you have to admit, things are a little downtrodden." He told him he'd help. "Good. Next thing I wanted to talk to you about is the grocery store. Your mom tells me that the shelves are about always empty, and there isn't but two people working there most of the time. Last week she had to wait on the cashier to finish slicing deli stuff before she could check out. I think we can see about that as well."

"Ask Dane about that. I mean, she's going to be taking on a project that I was emailed about, looking into seeing why their production is down. Maybe this will be right up her alley." His dad asked about the project. "I'm not sure what he thought I could do, but apparently I was recommended by someone to help him out. I guess he's losing money on how things are running. She said she'd do it."

"I'll talk to her. She's got a good head on her shoulders. Perhaps it's nothing more than a little cash flow trouble for both places." Brayden didn't think so, but he had no idea about production lines or grocery stores. "Levi is talking like he wants to move into one of the buildings in town. A studio. I think that's a good idea too. Give him some room and a place he can be as messy as he wants."

"Mom said that he has another show coming up. Do you think he'll go to this one?" Levi was a very famous painter, but he was also a recluse. He preferred staying at home and working rather than going out in public. He even had his groceries delivered to his house. And a person came in once a week to make him dinners and put them in the freezer for him. He did not like people.

"He said that he'd rather have someone cut off his nose than to have to go to one of these things. Last time, your mother and I went. It was funny for us to hear how the people were speculating about this painter and his work. We both got a big laugh thinking how if only these people knew what a slob he was, and he wasn't an old man like they thought. People. They are very strange at times, aren't they?" Brayden agreed with him.

Tillman said he'd make sure that there was dinner for them all in an hour if they wanted to stay. The rest of his brothers said they could make it, but Christian had to leave early as he had a court date in the morning. Wyatt said that he had a woman that was due today, but that he was sure she wouldn't deliver until next week.

By the time dinner was called, they were all having a good time. Not that they didn't normally, but they each seemed to be more relaxed and laid back than he'd seen them in a while. There was talk about the picnic that he and Dad were planning. Mom talked about the county fair and what was going on there. The evening flew by, and he was in bed with Dane at his side when he realized how much he loved his family.

"I'm sure that you have always loved them." He pulled her to his body and Dane curled around him. "They're really different than most families. The ones that I've been around are always picking at each other. Arguing about this or that.

179

Mostly money. But this family, they seem to need each other. Desperately."

"I think in a way we do." He pulled her up over his hips and took her shirt off. "I'd very much like it if you helped work some of the soreness out of me. My cock feels very sore and full." She moved down his thighs. As she took his cock into her hands, he nearly came when she cupped his balls. "You keep that up and you're going to be very disappointed when I come and you don't."

"I'm not worried. You'll satisfy me when I want it." He said that his cat wanted to as well. "I'd like that as well, but first I want to taste you."

Brayden rolled her to her back and pulled her panties off. She asked him what he was doing when he let his cat take him. He'd been patient long enough, Brayden thought, and he needed his mate.

CHAPTER 13

Dane screamed out her release. It was that, she thought, or explode. His cat was eating her like a last meal, devouring her as if she was a feast. Her body felt worshiped. Loved. And most of all cherished. As she came again, this time begging him to let her breathe, he moved over her leg and licked her thigh. She knew what he was going to do just seconds before he clamped his teeth deeply into her flesh.

This time her scream was one of pain. But almost as soon as it took her breath away, the pain faded away and became nothing more than what a bruise felt like when bumped. When the cat let her go, his tongue lapped over the wound twice before she felt the tightness of magic, and then she had her Brayden back. He held her, telling her that he loved her.

"I love you too. Please. I need for you to finish me." He laughed. "Well, what did you expect me to be, pissy? I might be if I don't get to come with you. And right now."

He made love to her with his hands and his mouth. Everywhere he touched her, she felt marked by his love. And when he slid into her, his cock caressed her too. Holding onto Brayden, Dane knew that she'd found her only love. The man who would love her for the rest of her days.

They came together as only a mated couple could. Loving each other, making the other feel special. And he was to her. He would be for the rest of their days. She loved Brayden Stanton with all that she was.

When her climax took her, she cried out with it. Brayden's name and her love for him. When he came, filling her with his seed, she felt it as it warmed her body from the inside out. Her heart filled with so much love that she knew he had felt it too.

Afterwards, they held each other, not speaking. There wasn't any need for words now, and she enjoyed the quiet of the house. It was a perfect one too, she thought. Big enough to fill when they wanted, and roomy enough to find a place to hide out when quiet time was necessary. Dane rolled to her side and looked at Brayden.

"I want to have a child." He kissed her on the mouth and then pulled her atop him. "Now? I thought we'd wait a couple of days."

"You're not ready yet." It took her a moment to figure out what he was saying. "I mean, you could be. I'm not entirely sure what your body does. But you don't smell like you're in heat. That's the only way that I can impregnate you. But if you'd not mind, I'd really like for us to be married first. I know that we're mates, but I want to make it legal in everyone's eyes."

"I don't have anyone. I mean, no family that would care. I know that your family is aware that we're mates, so it matters little to them either." He said she had family. "No. When I was younger, my parents were killed in a horrific car accident. It took my older brother and little sister too. I was staying with my grandma. She's since passed on as well."

"You have five brothers, and a set of parents who all love you as much as I do. You have an already built in family." She hugged him to her. "They do love you. I think you scare them a little, but they do."

"And I love them."

Exhaustion took her then. Brayden had a way of wearing her out and she loved that too. She knew that he slept as well; the soft snoring beside her was like a ticking clock, comforting.

"Good morning." It seemed as if she'd only closed her eyes for a moment when he kissed her. Blinking the sleep out of her eyes as he held her, she felt like she'd slept well but could have used a bit more. They continued to lay there for several more minutes until Brayden said that he had to get up. "Allie is here today. I nearly forgot. She told me yesterday that she likes things orderly and on time. I can't make her pissy again." Dane was laughing when he got up to head to the shower. When he paused, she looked at him. "I have to hit her. I don't feel right doing that. But she told me I had until today to get over the macho shit. I'm not sure I'll ever get over it."

"She'll make sure you do. If you don't, then she'll beat you senseless until you do. Someday you might have to hit a woman. If you don't, it could get you killed." He said he understood that, but she wasn't his enemy. "She might be if you don't show her you can do it."

When he left to go to his training, she took her shower. It was nice not having to worry about being hurt for a change. And to have someone around to make her feel better when she was. Dane looked down at the scar on her leg and was surprised to see that the bite from this morning was scarred over as well.

It was a perfect impression of the cat's teeth, both on the top of her thigh and under it. She ran her fingers over it and could feel her cat, one that she didn't use all that often, stirring over her. She wondered if she'd begin using her more now that she was a mate to one.

Yesterday the tech guys had come in and set up her computer in the office, as well as Brayden's. There was a jumper on both lines, but hers took longer to trace. Whenever she was on the

Internet, the ping of her IP address would bounce all over the world for forty minutes before it came back to her. And it would change routes each time she used it along different points. It was a way to keep them all safe. Brayden's would bounce for twenty, but he assured her that he understood the importance of using it for only that time frame.

She pulled up her email then and saw that she had three emails from Walter and one from the man she was going to help with his production line. She was more excited about that than she was the job with Walter. While she was going over the email that she'd printed up from Mr. Landon, Denny came in the room with a thick file.

"This is the information that I could get on the grocery store. Brayden said he'd talk to you about it." Dane nodded and took the file. "For the last several months the shelves have been almost empty. I'm not sure what's going on, but when I asked about it and the understaffing, I was told it was in transition. I haven't been able to find out what that means either."

She looked on the Internet and found it. "They're on the market to be sold. To a larger chain, I would imagine. There is no deal on the table yet. More than likely waiting on them to lower their price. I'm thinking that they're going to close this one down in order to stop the competition." Denny asked her how much they were wanting. After telling him the amount, Dane looked at him. "What you should do is bail them out. Buy it, and then you can help them get back on their feet. Or sell to the highest bidder when the time comes. They have no offer, which means they'll more than likely take what you suggest."

"I'll call Christian." After ten minutes of talking to his son, Denny hung up. "Do you know how to run a grocery store?"

"No. But the manager might stay on if you pay him to help you out for a few months. Or you could get a consultant. I'd go that route if I were you, simply because if the manager is a failure at it, then you don't want more of the same."

"I agree. I don't know that we need one of those big grocery stores here. But we do need one. Just for the convenience of those who don't drive or have the means to pay those prices." She nodded, looking over the paperwork that he'd given her. "You can see there that they're behind in a few of their bills. Do you suppose it's because of the lack of food or that other things are going on?"

"Both. As I said, this Jacob Mann, he's been losing money for a few years now. I'd say it has more to do with him than the economy. People do have to eat, so that might only be a part of it." She was ready to close the file when she saw something that caught her eye. "Denny, did you know that you own the land that this store is on?"

"No. Are you sure?" He came to the desk and she showed him the paperwork. "That would have been my daddy. He owned a great deal of land here before the town started to grow. I wonder why no one ever told me that before?"

"I would say that it's because anyone knowing you would have figured you were aware of it. You're a very smart man and someone that is organized. If you can buy the store, you'll be in a better position if you do want to sell later. That might be why there has been no bids on the place. They can own the store but would be paying you rent." He sat back down but looked less than convinced. "What is it?"

"I should have known that was my land. I mean, I could have done something before now." She said that he might not have been able to. "Of course, but I wonder why no one said anything. I mean, my daddy has been dead for some time. You think it was a mistake then?"

"I don't know, Denny. I mean, there is no point in

185

borrowing trouble if you don't have to. And if later on you find out differently, you can act then. But you know now, so that's a good thing."

Within the hour, Denny owned the store. She told him now that it was settled, there would be others coming to him to buy it because he was the full owner.

"All right then. I don't want to sell for now, but I'll keep that in mind. I don't need the money, none of us do, but it might be something that I can't turn down." She told him to keep an open mind about it and to not sell to the first bidder. "I won't. I can see that would be a mistake. Thank you very much for your help. I would have mucked it up."

"I doubt that. Like I said, you're a smart man." She asked him about the guy who had called about production troubles. "Would you like to go with me? I can go alone, but if you want to hang out today, I'd like that."

"I think I'd enjoy that. And maybe, if you allow me to, I'll buy you some lunch while we're out. Lucy has that girly thing going on today. I call it that because it annoys her. She's trying to get some rose starts as well while she's out." He looked so sad. "I'm surely sorry that woman did that, but I think Lucy is happy to be starting again. Not long ago she told me that she wished that she'd planned the garden better. This will be a good new beginning for her."

~~~

Allie watched the big man fall back. He did it well...still tried to stop himself with his hands, but he was getting better at rolling with the fall rather than trying to stop it. When she told him to try again, she waited while the other brothers got into position. This was the most fun she'd had in a while. And the most respect that she'd ever gotten from a client. Glancing to her right, she saw that Perry looked to be having as much fun as she was with Mrs. Stanton at the firing range. These people sure knew how to make a place work for them.

"This time I want you to think about how you're falling. I know that you can pretty much land on your feet, and that you're a cat so you'll heal quickly, but think about how you're leaving yourself unprotected for whoever is trying to hurt you." Brayden asked her what she meant. "All right. Is your heart exposed? Are you giving this person a clear shot at your chest? Do you have any way for you to leap back up, say land on your feet almost as soon as you fall? What's close to you when you go down? Anything you can use for shelter if need be? These are things you have to be aware of once you're down. And things that you have to think of every time you have someone after you."

They were working through the movements when she noticed that a car had pulled into the driveway. She ignored it for the most part, but did keep her eye on the people that hadn't gotten out yet. Just as she was going to ask Brayden who it might be, she saw Levi take a hard fall and went to see if he was all right.

There was blood on his arm that came from a scrape on his hand. Also, he was going to have a huge bruise from the large rock he'd landed on. When he started to laugh, she knew that he was more embarrassed than hurt.

"You're not cut too badly." He thanked her and let her help him up. Before she could get him cleared of the ground, he was simply gone.

The big cougar was circling Levi. And when he leaped at him, Levi shifted as well. They were at each other so quickly and so viciously that she stepped forward to stop them. But Brayden stopped her before she could get too close.

"They'll hurt you and not realize it." She said they were

hurting each other. "Yes. But they can heal, you cannot. Just wait— Well, shit."

She had no idea what was going on, but watching the two cats tear at each other made her think this wasn't going to end well for anyone. Brayden was of no help. He walked away from her, laughing hard enough that he had to lean on trees to keep his balance. Allie had had enough and pulled out her gun.

Firing twice at the cats, she heard one of them scream. The second cat, she had no idea which was which any more, came at her. Lifting her gun up again, she told him to stop.

"I'll kill you. I have no idea what set you off, but don't think for a moment that I won't pull the trigger." No one moved, not even the cat. "Who the fuck are you?"

He shifted. The man standing before her, the very naked man, looked good enough to eat, but she didn't lower her weapon. And when he cut the distance between them in half, she told him once again to stop.

"You're my mate. I was only going to come here and tease my brothers, but I could smell you and I knew." She didn't have any idea what that meant, but he came at her again. "Put that down before you hurt someone. I said you're my mate, damn it. I don't have time to explain every little thing to you. This could not have come at a worse time in my life."

"Well la dee da. I'm not stopping this.... Can you fucking put some clothing on?" He said no, he liked it this way. "I see. Actually, I don't. This mate thing, it makes you stupid, right? Something about your mind being half what it normally is."

"No. I'm fully capacitated. Why don't you put that gun down and I'll explain things to you?" That set her off and she fired a shot between his feet. "What the fuck are you doing? I told you to put that damned thing down."

Someone cleared their throat and she didn't look. But the

man did. He looked like he was flushing, but it was the way he covered himself, or tried to, that piqued her curiosity. He was large…even when not erect she could see that he was a well-endowed man. Then when the person began to speak, she took a moment to look over his body. Damn, but he was a fine looking man, she thought.

"You think you're going to get very far talking to her like a simpleton?" Brayden. Or she thought. The voice sounded older, and then she realized it was his dad. "Why don't you come away now, Christian, and get dressed. Cooler heads will prevail, you know."

"Dad, I could smell her as soon as I came up the yard. And Levi was touching her." She couldn't have heard that right. Touching her? "He should know better. I told him to keep away."

"Who the hell are you?" He told her his name. "I don't give a shit about that. I mean, who the hell are you that you think you can tell me when people can touch me? Not to mention, telling me to do anything. I'm a big girl and I make my own decisions."

"You're my mate." She told him he kept saying that but it meant nothing to her. "It should. I'm going to be your husband too. And I'll say who touches you or not."

She'd had enough, and thought about turning and leaving him there to fend for himself. But at the last minute, he made a lunge for her and she fired. Allie was taken to the ground just as she heard someone crying out in pain.

Before You Go...

HELP AN AUTHOR

write a review

THANK YOU!

Share your voice and help guide other readers to these wonderful books. Even if it's only a line or two your reviews help readers discover the author's books so they can continue creating stories that you'll love. Login to your favorite retailer and leave a review. Thank you.

AWARD WINNING, BESTSELLING AUTHOR

Kathi Barton, winner of the Pinnacle Book Achievement award as well as a best-selling author on Amazon and All Romance books, lives in Nashport, Ohio with her husband Paul. When not creating new worlds and romance, Kathi and her husband enjoy camping and going to auctions. She can also be seen at county fairs with her husband who is an artist and potter.

Her muse, a cross between Jimmy Stewart and Hugh Jackman, brings her stories to life for her readers in a way that has them coming back time and again for more. Her favorite genre is paranormal romance with a great deal of spice. You can visit Kathi online and drop her an email if you'd like. She loves hearing from her fans. aaronskiss@gmail.com.

Follow Kathi on her blog: http://kathisbartonauthor.blogspot.com/